# contents

## SPRING/SUMMER 2018

## columns

## short fiction

## features

MW00491179

SPRING/SUMMER 2018

# saddlebag DISPATCHES

volume 4 • number 1

www.saddlebagdispatches.com

## staff

Dusty Richards, *publisher*
Casey W. Cowan, *publisher*
Venessa Cerasale, *admin director*
Michael Frizell, *editor-in-chief*
Dennis W. Doty, *managing editor*
Gil Miller, *associate editor*
Jeremy Menefee, *associate editor*
Gordon Bonnet, *associate editor*
George "Clay" Mitchell, *features writer*
Cyndy Prasse Miller, *features writer*
Patricia Rustin-Christen, *photographer*
Vivian Cummings, *marketing director*
Andrew Butters, *webmaster*

## contributors

Rod Miller • Terry Alexander
John T. Biggs • John J. Dwyer
Velda Brotherton • Chet Dixon
Richard Prosch • Michael McLean
Elaine Marze • George Gilland
Laurie Muirhead • John M. Floyd
Steven Carr • D.A. Frizell

## advertising

For advertising rates and
information, please contact:

Venessa Cerasale, Admin Director
venessa@oghmacreative.com

For art guidelines and
ad submissions, please contact:

Vivian Cummings, Marketing Director
vivian@oghmacreative.com

# saddlebag DISPATCHES

WHERE STORIES OF THE WEST COME TO BE TOLD

# Submission Guidelines

*We are now taking submissions for our Autumn/Winter, 2018 issue
dedicated to all things rodeo due out in mid-December, 2018.*
**DEADLINE IS AUGUST 1, 2018**

Galway and Tiree Press are Oghma Creative Media's western and historical imprints, and *Saddlebag Dispatches* is our semi-annual flagship publication. We are looking for short stories, serial novels, poetry, and non-fiction articles about the west. These will have themes of open country, unforgiving nature, struggles to survive and settle the land, freedom from authority, cooperation with fellow adventurers, and other experiences that human beings encounter on the frontier. Traditional westerns are set west of the Mississippi River and between the end of the American Civil War and the turn of the twentieth century. But the western is not limited to that time. The essence, though, is openness and struggle. These are happening now as much as they were in the years gone by.

**QUERY LETTER:** Put this in the e-mail message: In the first paragraph, give the title of the work, and specify whether it is fiction, poetry, or nonfiction. If the latter, give the subject. The second paragraph should be a biography between one hundred and two hundred words.

**MANUSCRIPT FORMATTING:** All documents must be in Times New Roman, twelve-point font, double spaced, with one-inch margins all around. Do not include extra space between paragraphs. Do not write in all caps, and avoid excessive use of italics, bold, and exclamation marks. Files must be in .doc, .docx, or .rtf format. Fiction manuscripts should be in standard manuscript format. For instructions and examples see https://www.shunn.net/format/story.html. Submit the entire and complete fiction or poetry manuscript. We will consider proposals for non-fiction articles.

**OTHER ATTACHMENTS:** Please also submit a picture of yourself and any pictures related to your manuscript. All photos must be high-resolution (at least 300 dpi) and include a photo caption and credit, if necessary.

Manuscripts will be edited for grammar and spelling. Submit to
**submissions@saddlebagdispatches.com,** with your name in the subject line.

AN AMERICAN LEGEND

DUSTY RICHARDS

1937-2018

# five beans in the
# WHEEL

**Casey W. Cowan**
*saddlebag dispatches publisher*

The vast majority of you don't know me, but I was Dusty Richards's business partner in this enterprise known as *Saddlebag Dispatches*. He was the living legend, the face of the operation. I, on the other hand, was the guy with the laptop in the back room putting it all together. If you're into spy or super-hero movies at all, you could say I was Dusty's "Guy in the Chair"—and I've had few greater privileges in my life.

Things are different now. What do you do when you're a master of words—a publisher of them, even—but none will come to describe the hole inhabiting your heart? What do you do when your stock-in-trade can't come close to conveying the depths of emptiness and despair at the loss of someone you looked up to more than almost anyone?

You keep going. You keep typing. You keep doing the one thing that your mentor admonished you to do above all other things—you keep writing.

They say that a child doesn't come into his or her own unless and until the death of their father. If that's the case, we as a company were shoved into adulthood four months ago when we learned of Dusty's passing. Our friend. Our partner. Our mentor. Our father.

Keep writing.

What can we say about Dusty? The *real* question is what *can't* we say about him? To observe that he was larger than life is the grandest of understatements. He was an irresistible force and an unmovable object all rolled into one, a personality wider than the western

skies he wrote about. He was an eternal optimist, a man who woke up each and every day renewed and ready for the next job, the next challenge, the next good fight. He was a father, a patriarch, a mentor of the first order. He toured the country teaching and encouraging new and experienced writers alike, challenging them to follow his lead, tell the next inspiring story, pen the next Great American Novel. He was a fighter, a lover, a joker, an entrepreneur, a canny businessman, a television and radio personality, a famous rodeo announcer, a cowboy, and, perhaps above all else, a master storyteller.

He kept writing.

Dusty was everything under his trademark ten-gallon hat and so much more, and we could keep writing for a year and not do him justice. He was a legend, and one that touched the lives of many, many thousands—possibly millions—of people.

But now the great man has passed on, and it's time to go to back to work.

To keep writing.

Since starting this business five years ago, I've lost several people who have meant the world to me, be it through death or simply the ever-shifting tides of life. While these loved ones are gone, I keep the memory of them close to my heart, grateful for every moment I got to spend with them, and always striving to honor the influence they had upon me. As I reluctantly take up the reins as the new Publisher of *Saddlebag Dispatches*, in his stead, I will do the same for Dusty.

I'll keep writing.

But I'm not Dusty. I can never replace him, nor would I try. I can only follow in his footsteps and do my best to act as he would. And as he would probably say, those are some pretty damn big boots to fill... and I don't even own a pair of boots.

I do, however, have a *hat.* A cowboy hat. *Dusty's* hat.

A few weeks after his funeral, one of our fellow writers wrote an amazing eulogy to our dear, departed Ranch Boss talking about the old hat of Dusty's he'd won a couple of years ago, how big it is, and how it's a reminder to him of what he's doing as a writer and why. As a protégé of Dusty, I knew instantly what he was talking about. So I asked Dusty's family if I, too, could have one of his old hats to remember him by. His daughters graciously agreed, and brought me a stunning black dress hat a few days later at a conference.

I ended up carrying that hat around all day. It captured me. I'd been feeling lost since Dusty's passing—unfocused, angry, guilty, depressed, and very, very sad. And suddenly, I was holding something in my hand that very firmly connected me back to him. It was like a clear-skied dawn after a night of storms. Instead of focusing on myself and my sense of loss, I finally remembered the *man*, what he was all about, and the faith he had in me. There are so many paths we can choose in this life, so many rabbit holes, obstacles, sinkholes, detours, traps... they're simply unavoidable.

We need to keep writing.

We can either get bogged down in them feeling sorry for ourselves, or we can deal with the task at hand and keep our eyes on the prize. Dusty always, *ALWAYS*, did the latter, no matter how bad things got. And that may be his final, greatest lesson to us all. In life—as in writing—you never give up, never forget who you are or what you want, or that a little hard work and elbow grease will get you there, no matter what anybody thinks or says.

Dusty's hat now lives on a shelf in my office. When I look at it, I feel like the Boss is still right here with

CASEY, DUSTY, AND FELLOW AUTHOR RANDALL DALE AT THE WILL ROGERS MEDALLION AWARDS BANQUET IN FORT WORTH, TEXAS IN OCTOBER, 2016. DUSTY AND RANDALL BOTH WALKED AWAY WITH MEDALS THAT NIGHT.

me, looking over my shoulder as I work, pointing out corrections here and there as we created this magazine. I remember that he had faith in me and my talents, and that he had every intention of one day passing me the torch to continue his work helping and inspiring

A LIGHT MOMENT DURING THE MAY, 2014 **OZARKS WRITERS LEAGUE** CONFERENCE IN BRANSON, MISSOURI,

**CASEY, DUSTY,** AND *LONGMIRE* CREATOR **CRAIG JOHNSON** AT THE **WESTERN WRITERS OF AMERICA** CONFERENCE IN CHEYENNE, WYOMING IN JUNE, 2016.

writers to become authors, and keeping the spirit of the West alive in today's collective conscience. I just sorely wish that that baton hadn't been passed quite so soon.

For obvious reasons, then, this issue of *Saddlebag Dispatches* is dedicated to the memory of the late, great Dusty Richards, as well as to his lovely wife Pat, and their family. It will mark a new era in the short history of our publication, but one that will carry on the traditions and ethics Dusty instilled in us over the long haul.

We'll keep writing.

As mentioned above, I will be taking over Dusty's seat as Publisher, overseeing all aspects of the magazine and its business, and, for the time being, its production. I will be joined by our very able new Editor-in-Chief, Michael L. Frizell, and our new Managing Editor, Dennis Doty. They will oversee day-to-day management of submissions and the Editorial Department, aided by Associate Editors Jeremy Menefee, Gil Miller, and Gordon Bonnet, and Feature Writers George "Clay" Mitchell and Cyndy Prasse Miller. Venessa Cerasale runs our Business Department, including advertising sales, Vivian Cummings supervises Marketing, and Patricia Rustin Christen

remains our Chief Photographer. We will continue to publish on a semi-annual basis for the foreseeable future—June and December—and continue bringing you the best in Western-themed fiction, poetry, history, events, and culture. This is our promise to you... and Dusty.

As for Dusty, I'm certain that he's sitting around that big ol' campfire in the sky right now, Pat at his side, swapping stories with the likes of Zane Grey, Louis L'Amour, and his old friends Jory Sherman and Cotton Smith. He was not one for self-pity, grief, or taking his foot off the gas for a second. He wouldn't want to be grieved, but celebrated. He'd want us to keep his memory alive by following his lead. By chasing the sunset with all that we've got, pursuing our dream, living with passion, and cherishing the ones we love. And that's what we'll do, how we'll honor our beloved father. Keep fighting. Keep telling stories. Keep doing what Dusty did until we can't anymore.

Keep writing,
Casey W. Cowan
*Publisher*

*biscuits and tenderfoot for*

# BREAKFAST

**Michael L. Frizell**

*saddlebag dispatches editor-in-chief*

S purred by my fascination with science fiction, I learned to read earlier than most. My father, a laborer, understood education's power and encouraged my voracious appetite for words by supplying copies of Starlin's *Warlock* and *The Phantom Stranger* and purchasing any pulp paperback I wanted, age-appropriateness be damned. On the rare occasion, I was approached by a member of the perfumed sex as a teen, the vast vocabulary lent to me by reading a steady diet of Blatty, Brooks, King, and Clarke failed me in spectacular ways. Words didn't fail me when I experienced my first brush with publication when Marvel printed my short story/letter in issue number forty of *ROM: Spaceknight.* The letter didn't score me phone numbers, but I was able to hold my head a little higher. My favorite comic had recognized my work.

Since then, I've obtained four degrees, two of those include advanced degrees in writing, and have worked as a professor and administrator in higher education for eighteen years. I've published in several venues and serve as the editor of a peer-reviewed journal, *The Learning Assistance Review.* Thanks to Tidal Wave Comics, I was able to realize my dream of writing comic books, and have been trusted with their largest, licensed character, Bettie Page. I've written sanctioned comic books for politicians like Elizabeth Warren, musicians, and actors. I've written custom comics for production companies and a famous actor. My first published comic, *Tribute: Christopher Reeve,* was supported by the Reeve Foundation. It was an honor that has left me wanting more.

My background as a writer likely differs from most who work as editors of western-themed magazines such

as *Saddlebag Dispatches,* but it is a role I believe I've been training for since I was a shy kid who devoured every comic he found on the spinner rack at his local Piggly Wiggly. As an academic, I'm used to deadlines and required to publish. What better way to meet this mandate than by embracing one of the mediums I love most?

Every decision, good or bad, sane or crazy, you have ever made has brought you to where you are right now, this second. You are the sum of every experience, every joy, every sad-ness, every heartbreak, every make-out session, every-thing. You've heard the cliché, "Life is what happens when you're making other plans," right? I'd like to modify that some.

I say, "Life is what happens when you're making other plans and you're smart and open-minded enough to take full advantage of the experiences offered." The simple answer to this question is that I couldn't pass up an opportunity to join this publication.

Like every creative person, I'm looking for "my

tribe" of like-minded people to talk about writing. As I've matured (a debatable descriptor for someone who writes comic books and graphic novels, but I digress), I've recognized both the need for advocating for a genre that is beloved by fans, embraced by adventure-lovers, and universally recognized as a powerful medium for telling stories unique to the American experience.

> AS AN **ACADEMIC**, I'M USED TO **DEADLINES** AND **REQUIRED TO PUBLISH**. WHAT BETTER WAY TO MEET THIS MANDATE THAN BY EMBRACING ONE OF THE **MEDIUMS I LOVE** MOST?

Thank you for reading this short essay, *Saddle-bag Dispatches,* and all of the superior work published through Oghma Creative Media's various imprints. I look forward to riding with you through the fictional and nonfictional stories that create an exciting tapestry that is the American West.

Yippee-ki-yay,
Michael Frizell
*Editor-in-Chief*

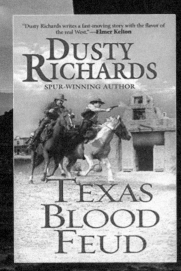
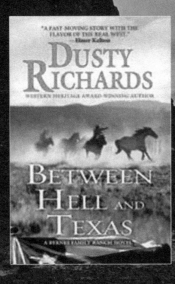
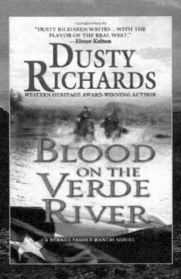
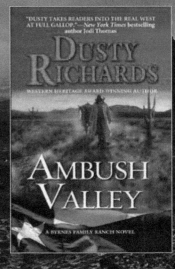
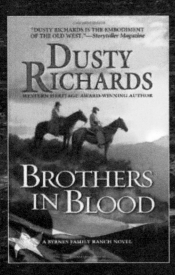
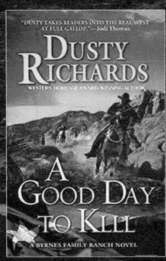
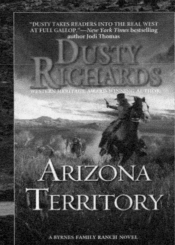
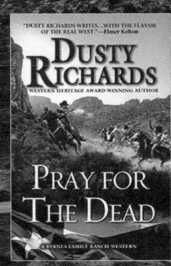
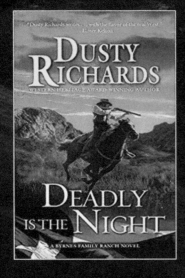
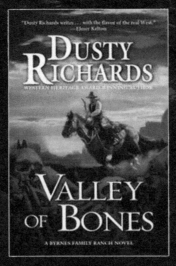
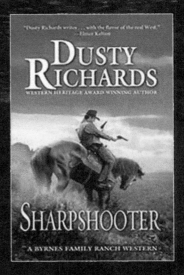

# THE AWARD-WINNING
# BRANDIRON SERIES

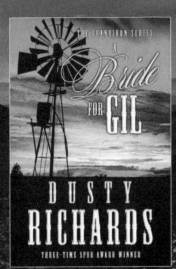

**2016**
**WILL ROGERS**
**MEDALLION**

SILVER MEDALIST
BEST WESTERN
ROMANCE

**2017**
**WESTERN WRITERS**
**OF AMERICA**

SPUR AWARD WINNER
BEST WESTERN
TRADITIONAL NOVEL

## AND THE ADVENTURES CONTINUE...

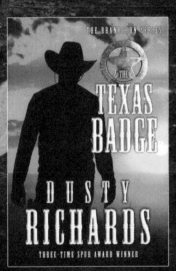

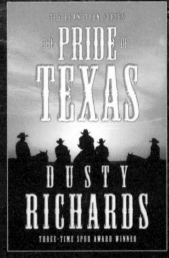

# DUSTY RICHARDS
## THREE-TIME SPUR AWARD WINNER

## Chet Dixon
*saddlebag dispatches poet*

Stormy times are part of our lives. We always dread them and sometimes suffer a long aftermath. Recently, our family here at *Saddlebag Dispatches* experienced a terrible storm with the passing of the great Dusty Richards and his wife, Pat. Troubled waters rose around our friends, but we were unable to do anything substantial to help them and their family.

Helplessness is something none of us likes feeling. But what can we really do when people we love are in dire straits like these? The first and continuous help we can give is prayer. Though pain, fear, and disorder have overcome them, we each can pray that God will give them comfort,

courage, healing, and a spirit of hope. Prayer can transform a torn and worn body to again go forward on the many miles they have yet to go.

This horrible accident that Dusty and his wife have experienced should help us all realize how important friendships are. For many years, our friend Dusty has shared knowledge and wisdom about how to pursue and reach our dreams. He has shared his talents, skills and methods eagerly and freely propelling many of us forward at a rate not possible alone.

Times like this inspire me to write my thoughts. By sharing them, my wish is that they will give help, comfort, and hope.

*—Chet Dixon is a businessman, philanthropist, and published author of multiple works, including the poetry collections* Beyond the Trailhead *and* Affections Not Sleeping. *He resides near Branson, Missouri, but his heart lives in the western wilderness.*

## A FRIEND IN NEED

We are often blessed by persons unaware
They are being watched as secret mentors.
For them we owe great debts
As we reap the profits and keep seeking more.

Sometimes these mentors never know
They helped us outlast doubts and fears
And encouraged us to be relentless
when overcoming trouble
Through tiresome sweat and tears.

When they taught us in sincere ways
They left no doubt about unfulfilled dreams.
Wake up!   Stand up!   Hurry on!  they advised.
The great world you seek is still downstream.
The rapids you face may be rough and turbid.
Fear and troubles may lurk at every bend.
But they will say, move on down,
Troubles are normal before an end.

Now after years receiving gifts they offer
We give our help to ford their rapids ahead.
Until they stand tall again and walk alone,
We will be their crutch and lend a helping hand.

# HEROES & OUTLAWS

**Velda Brotherton**

*historical columnist*

It's difficult to believe that the peaceful town of Ft. Smith, Arkansas was once about as wild as the west could get. Its wide streets and quiet outlying neighborhoods are far removed from those days when gunplay was a regular event and ladies of the evening openly plied their trade. Hard to imagine Ft. Smith as a gateway to the wildest of the wild west. Indian Territory lay just across the Arkansas River. A haven for the worst of the worst, it would one day take Judge Isaac Parker, the man known as "The Hanging Judge," to tame things down.

SITUATED AT THE CONFLUENCE OF THE ARKANSAS AND POTEAU RIVERS, **FORT SMITH** WOULD BECOME AN IMPORTANT **FRONTIER FORT**. IT WAS FIRST ESTABLISHED AS AN OUTPOST IN 1817 WHEN **MAJOR WILLIAM BRADFORD** AND HIS COMMAND PUT ASHORE ON THE ROCK LANDING BELOW **BELLE POINT**.

But let's go back to the very beginning when the settlement was little more than a rocky point above a wide, muddy river. Situated at the confluence of the Arkansas and Poteau rivers, Fort Smith would become a most important frontier fort. It was first established as an outpost in 1817 when Major William Bradford and his command of 64 men put ashore on the rock landing below Belle Point. One of Bradford's duties was to prevent the Indians from continuing hostilities with each other. He and his small troop would face thousands of Indians fighting each other. They would not hesitate to face down a few white men in uniforms.

Due to the remote location, the tiny army was pretty much on its own. They were to erect a post on the Arkansas near the point where the Osage boundary struck the river. The first few rude shelters built there by Major Stephen Long of the Topographical Engineers, before Bradford's arrival, were designated as Camp Smith in honor of General Thomas Smith, commander of the 9th Military Department with headquarters at Belle Fontaine. On hearing that Bradford was on his way, Long left his plans for the first fort along with a small detail of men and went on his exploratory way.

Hostilities that began in 1808 between the native Osage tribe and the foreign latecomers, the Cherokee, would eventually lead to Bradford's heroic actions. A delegation of Cherokee chiefs from East Tennessee had visited then-President Thomas Jefferson and asked that he allow members of their tribe to live as hunters and emigrate to the lands west of the Mississippi River. At this time the Osage claimed all the land west of the Mississippi between the Missouri and Arkansas

Rivers. So this move could cause a war between those tribes. Yet, on January 9, 1809, President Jefferson authorized the requested move. Within a few years, a few thousand Cherokees had settled on the Arkansas and White Rivers in Arkansas. An emigration that occurred a good thirty years prior to the Trail of Tears that would herd thousands of more Cherokees out of their homelands and into Indian Territory to the west of Arkansas.

An imaginary boundary, drawn by United States Commissioners, did little to keep the warring Indians apart. Constant friction caused killings, the stealing

to keep the peace between the hostile tribes. What he did could not be imagined by his superiors or the warring tribes. Immediately he called a meeting of the leaders of the Shawnee, Delaware, Chickasaw, and the Choctaw bands that had sided with the Cherokees. Bradford also counseled the Quapaws and the Cherokees to live in peace.

But these weren't all the hostiles Bradford was forced to deal with. Trouble-making white outlaws, hearing of the wilderness settlement with little law enforcement filtered into the territory and added their violent behavior to the mix. In addition,

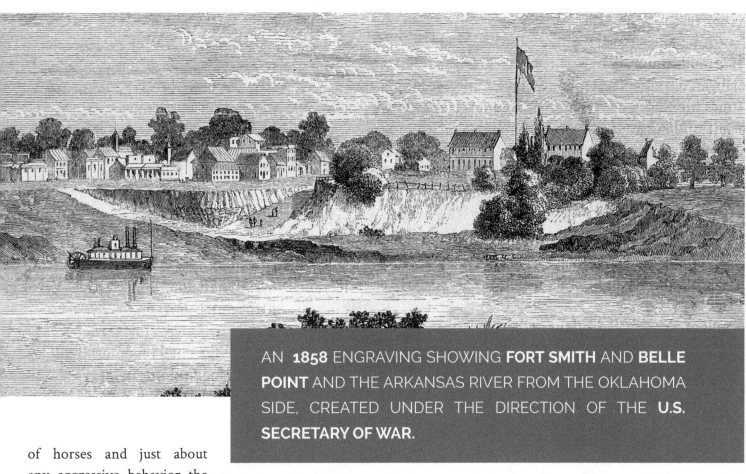

AN **1858** ENGRAVING SHOWING **FORT SMITH** AND **BELLE POINT** AND THE ARKANSAS RIVER FROM THE OKLAHOMA SIDE, CREATED UNDER THE DIRECTION OF THE **U.S. SECRETARY OF WAR.**

of horses and just about any aggressive behavior the Indians could come up with. The Treaty of Hiwassee of July 8, 1817, added more friction and gave the Cherokees as much land in Arkansas as they had relinquished in the Appalachian region. By then around 2,000 Cherokees lived in settlements on the Arkansas. By 1819, 3,500 to 6,000 lived there.

So then arrived Major Bradford and his company of Rifles to establish Fort Smith at Belle Point. Bradford had been ordered to do everything possible

frontier families squatted on Indian lands stirring up yet more trouble.

Faced with non-existent communication with Washington—it took up to three months or more for a message to reach Washington—decisions were left up to Bradford. As Indian wars flamed, he could only rely on his small company of blue and grey-clad Rifles and two six-pound cannons to handle the situations. Besides this, he had to keep a work

# JOHN J.
# DWYER

*Historical Fiction*

*Nonfiction*

**Author of**

*When the Bluebonnets Come*

*Robert E. Lee*

*Stonewall*

*War Between the States:*
*America's Uncivil War*

*The Oklahomans:*
*The Story of Oklahoma and Its Peop*

# w w w . j o h n j d w y e r . c o m

detail to plant corn and tend to a garrison vegetable garden. Because Congress had decided to be more frugal in army spending, most all of his supplies had to come from the soil. Hunting details also brought in wild game killed near the fort which gave the native Indians even more excuses to go on the warpath. To add to his problems were diseases known as the ague and bilious fever. During the summer of 1819, 100 Cherokees succumbed.

While Bradford was away a few Osage leaders, led by Bad Tempered Buffalo, and some 400 braves threatened the fort. Left in charge, Lt. Scott managed to hold down the uprising with just two cannon. By the time Bradford returned, it was rumored that over 1500 Osage warriors had amassed on the White River to take over the Cherokees' land. Bradford sent word this would not be tolerated. Then in a bold move, he warned the chiefs that if they shed one single drop of a white man's blood, he would exterminate their nations. He said he would not write Washington for advice or permission, but would simply report that there was not a Cherokee or Osage alive on his side of the Mississippi.

Bradford continued to work tirelessly to maintain an uneasy peace between the hostile tribes. At the end of his tour of duty in February, 1822, not one of his men had been killed by an Indian, and as far as was recorded, not one of his men had so much as fired a shot at one.

A new era began at Fort Smith with the arrival of Colonel Matthew Arbuckle who was convinced that the time was ripe to bring the Cherokees and the Osages together and restore a permanent peace on the Arkansas frontier. This could and did take a long while, but that's yet another story for another time.

*—Velda Brotherton is an award-winning nonfiction author, novelist, and a founding partner of* Saddlebag Dispatches. *She lives on a mountainside in Winslow, Arkansas, where she writes everyday and talks at length with her cat.*

# LEAN

*a poem by*

## LAURIE MUIRHEAD

The prairies can be voracious
vast stretch of needle grass and blue sky
consume cowboys on any given day
so much a part of this wild-scape
in love with the land, the space
and a good horse, they saddle-pack
minutes into hours into days and months
herding a system of values
not many know a damn thing about

Their drove of strong breeding and du-ability
left to the lean flank of skint soil
bring home a profit and winter flesh on their bones

Lean is all a cowboy knows
meagre meals, poor pay and the wind
hard from the west plays insanity
with the far border of a weak mind

A leaning tree on the lone savannah
doesn't know the straight side of tomorrow
and a crooked caballero at sundown
leans into the heat of the land
sleeps the saddle-side of a sore moon

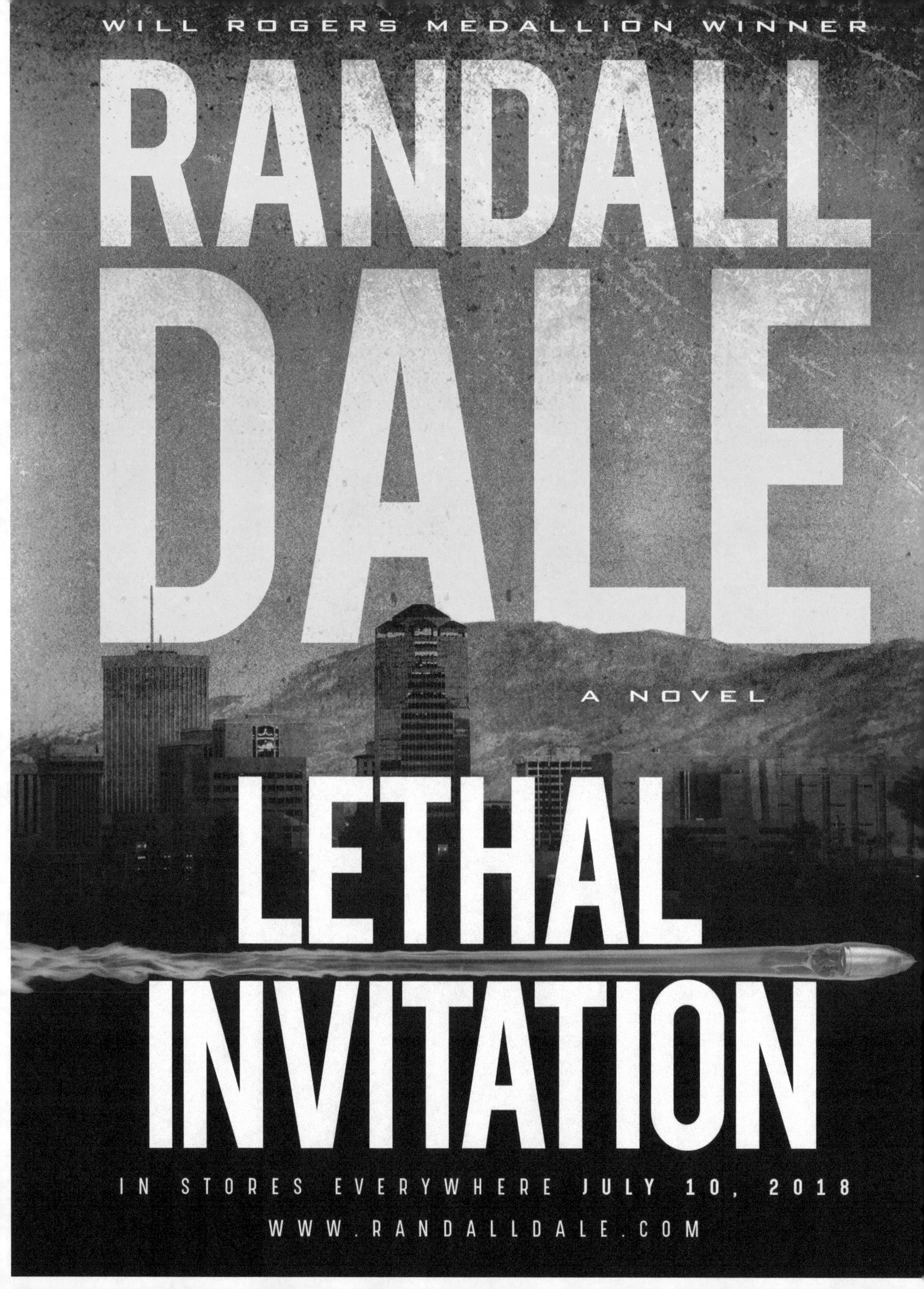
WILL ROGERS MEDALLION WINNER
RANDALL DALE
A NOVEL
LETHAL INVITATION
IN STORES EVERYWHERE JULY 10, 2018
WWW.RANDALLDALE.COM

# A SHORT STORY BY MICHAEL MCLEAN

# LITTLE THINGS

Dust billowed behind the white pickup as it traversed a series of creosote bush and mesquite-covered hills. Slowing at the crest of one rise, it bounced across a rusted cattle guard. Drooping strands of barbed wire clung to withered posts that stretched to the horizon in both directions. As Shannon Hall started down the dirt road, it became apparent that a fair-sized arroyo cut through the bottom of the valley ahead. Where the road crossed the arroyo, an old brown pickup stood idle alongside a sheriff's department truck, an SUV, and what looked like two dirt bikes. Several people gathered around the pickup.

Pulling in behind the SUV, she took a deep breath and drew a baseball cap down over short-cropped auburn hair. Intelligent grey eyes looked into the rearview mirror to make sure she appeared reasonably professional for the group now focused on her arrival. Satisfied, she pushed the door open and stepped into the hot desert afternoon. As a New Mexico Field Deputy Medical Investigator, this was where the work began.

Separating from the group, Sergeant Sam Jacobs greeted her. "Howdy, Doc. Ready for a short hike?"

Shannon smiled at the greeting. She wasn't a medical doctor, but once a few members of the Laguna County Sheriff's Department found out she had a doctorate in forensic archaeology, "Doc" had become her nickname. "Sure, Sam. What's going on?" she asked the older officer.

"Interesting situation. The kids here were spending their Saturday riding dirt bikes up and down these arroyos. They found the body and used a cell phone to call it in. Tommy got here about an hour ago, took a look, and called for us. I got here just a bit before you, and the rancher arrived somewhere in between. Tommy knows the rancher. Dated his daughter a while back."

Deputy Tommy Sanchez moved toward the duo. "Afternoon ma'am," he said in his usual jovial, but always respectful, manner. A decorated veteran of the conflict in Afghanistan, he was a local hero and youngest member of the sheriff's department.

"Hi, Tommy. Do you have details on this?"

Sam stepped back and allowed Sanchez to talk.

"These kids were running their bikes down the arroyo." He pointed at the motorcycle tracks in the sand. "About a quarter mile from here, a side drainage comes in. That's where the tall kid, Jamie Cooke, spotted boots and legs poking out of the mud and brush. They didn't mess with the scene and called 911." In a hushed voice, he added, "The other kid is Diné. You know, Navajo. He wants nothing to do with a dead person."

"What about him?" Shannon motioned toward the dour-looking man leaning on the pickup.

"Jim Iverson. He holds grazing rights for this land from the Bureau of Land Management." Sanchez led her over to the rancher and made introductions.

She had met several of his kind in southeastern New Mexico. It took a lot of hard work and a lot of acres to run a few dozen head of cattle and maybe some horses in dry country. The condition of the cattle guard and fencing confirmed her notion that the life of a rancher hereabouts was hard and getting ahead unlikely. Only a lucky few prospered when oil was discovered on their privately owned land.

"Mr. Iverson, I understand you got here after Deputy Sanchez?" she asked.

"That's right. I was coming back from checking on Willy Benson at the old line shack up by the north water tank when I spotted Tommy—uh, Deputy Sanchez—and these kids, so I stopped to see what was going on."

"Willy Benson? I haven't heard that name before."

"He travels around a lot," Iverson said. "Ed Benson and I were pretty tight until he passed on. Ed owned the neighboring ranch to the north… till the bank took it. Willy keeps to himself, so I let him stay up there. His daddy taught him to live off the land, you know, hunt and such. He makes pretty decent knives and fake Indian stuff to sell to tourists. I guess that's why he travels around." The rancher kicked at a chunk of limestone rock with a scuffed boot and stopped talking.

Ignoring the feeling that he didn't take to a female asking questions, Shannon merely smiled. "Thanks for the information."

Turning away, she motioned to Sam Jacobs. "Sam,

I'll go with Tommy and have a look. I'm guessing you'll want to stay here with Mr. Iverson and the boys and get their statements?"

"Love to," he replied, happy to expend minimal effort in the July heat.

—

**Scrunching through the sand** and gravel of the wash, with a backpack forensic kit slung over her shoulder, Shannon thought back to her first conversation with Sheriff Matt Gibson. After explaining that she had a doctorate in forensic archaeology and an undergraduate degree in criminal justice, she described owning a small consulting business to perform cultural or archeological assessments for resource companies and developers. However, a desire to be associated with law enforcement had prompted her to become a New Mexico Field Deputy Medical Investigator, or FDMI. The pool of FDMIs in Laguna County was small, but she had a passion for details and knew what was needed to understand and help resolve unusual or violent deaths. That was why FDMIs were called on scene to investigate and preserve evidence.

The sheriff had studied her for a few moments, and then asked why she would want to be in southeast New Mexico. Her answer was simple—family. Her grandparents had raised her and then retired to the north in Chavez County. He considered that, and then grinned. "It will be a pleasure for all of us to work with you, Miss Hall."

"Please, Shannon will do fine," she replied quickly, looking him straight in the eye. The words produced a wide smile on his weathered face.

Since that day, she had learned that the sheriff was an excellent judge of people. And, although elected to the position in part by the county's "good old boys," he was a respected and dedicated lawman. Gibson knew times weren't changing—they had changed. With his coaching, she had worked hard and quickly became the field deputy medical investigator of choice for crime scenes nobody else wanted.

Head down, absorbed in her reverie, she almost ran into Tommy Sanchez. They had arrived.

A pair of hiking boots protruded over a rocky drop-off three feet above the bottom of the arroyo proper. The body looked as if it had sluiced down the side drainage like a log and hung up on rocks as the water receded. Facedown, the remains were engulfed by sand and mud, obscured by tumbleweeds blown in by the ever-present wind. "Tommy, when was the last heavy rainfall around here?"

"Gosh, that would have been in April or early May. Had some real gullywashers, too. It's been darn dry ever since."

Shannon took out a notebook and looked at her watch. "I'm officially recording the time of death as of now."

"So noted, ma'am." Sanchez nodded as she made the official pronouncement as part of her duties.

Replacing the notebook, she began evaluating the scene and taking photos of the physical setting. Meanwhile, Sanchez pulled on a pair of work gloves and started to remove brush from around the lifeless form.

"Hold on, Tommy. Let me get organized here," she said.

Hoping to do something besides stand around, Sanchez spoke up. "I was going to move the brush since you already took a bunch of photos. The sun's not getting any higher."

Glancing at the position of the sun above the western horizon, she frowned and then reconsidered. "You're right. Go ahead. Just watch for anything unusual."

Even though she doubted much evidence would be preserved, if not found directly on the body, protocol dictated that she had to investigate and then make sure the body was properly packaged and transported to Albuquerque for autopsy.

Happy with the decision, Sanchez resumed work only to stop a few minutes later. "Uh, ma'am, I think you better see this."

The deputy had pulled weeds away from the body, exposing portions of the upper torso and trunk. Climbing up to Tommy's level, she looked where he was pointing. A partially open leather wallet stuck out of the hip pocket. Though dirty, sunlight reflected gold from the badge within.

Shannon Hall keyed the mike on her radio. "Sam, we have a real bad situation. Get word to Sheriff Gibson and let him know that it appears the deceased is a law enforcement officer, don't know whose yet. And let your office know we're going to need portable light generator sets, more deputies, and a lot of coffee. Hopefully the van from Albuquerque is rolling. This is going to take a while."

—

**Leaving a decent gravel** road behind, the truck crawled and bounced up a rough, rocky track so they could check out Iverson's statement about Willy Benson. Finally, the "line shack" materialized in the form of a thirty-foot-long, aluminum-sided trailer. Wondering how it got to this place stretched Shannon's imagination as much as believing that a person actually lived inside. Rusted, mostly indescribable stuff formed a sort of protective barrier around the trailer. A scattered handful of rusted cars and pickup trucks had long since merged with the desert. Only a beat-up Chevy baking in the sun suggested the possibility of life.

"Hello, the house," Sergeant Sam Jacobs called out. Moving a bit closer, he repeated the call. Suddenly, the door screeched open on rusting hinges and the enclosure belched a uniquely foul odor. Standing in the doorway, blinking rapid-fire in the bright light, a scruffy-looking man in his mid-thirties looked out at the pair.

"What do y'all want?" he asked in a surly tone.

"You Willy Benson?" Sam Jacobs asked, taking the lead.

The man nodded. "Yeah."

"We'd like to come in and ask you a few questions."

Shannon kept silent, observing everything, especially the man's body language.

"The place is a mess," Benson replied as he scratched at a thin, scabby arm extending from a sweat-stained tee shirt. "I been away for a while. Ain't had a chance to straighten things up."

"No problem," Jacobs said. "We see lots of untidy places. Yours is probably no worse."

Benson considered that for a few moments. "Well, I guess it'll be okay," he said, stepping back inside.

Jacobs followed cautiously, hand resting on his pistol, watching the man for any sign of movement toward a weapon, but he just plopped down on a worn out chair and leered at Shannon as she entered the trailer.

"You live here alone?" Jacobs asked, looking around and catching Shannon wrinkle her nose at the smell of the place.

"Yeah. Don't like people all that much."

"Your rancher friend, Iverson, says you're an artistic guy. You make Indian things to sell to tourists."

With what passed for a glimmer of pride, the man opened up a bit. "Yeah, that's where I been, out to Arizona and back selling to tourist traps and rock shops. City folks don't know the difference and kids like that sort of stuff. Here, take a look," he said, jumping up from the chair.

As Jacobs gripped his handgun, Shannon's hand instinctively slipped to the Smith & Wesson .40 caliber pistol she carried on such trips with the sheriff's team. But the man was only retrieving a small box from what served as a table.

He held out the box for them to see. Several pink and

grey arrowheads rested on a folded napkin. Surprised, she spoke for the first time. "Those are really well done, like small works of art. And you make them?"

"Yes, ma'am. I sit outside in the afternoon shade and work on them," he answered, still scratching his arm, an apparent side effect of methamphetamine use that also complemented his missing teeth.

Shannon again detected that hint of pride. His answer also explained the multitude of small rock chips she had observed when approaching the trailer. Peering into the box again, she noticed each arrowhead had two small notches in the middle of the base. She had seen a lot of arrowheads in her archaeological studies, but had never seen a style like that. "Are those little notches there on purpose?"

Benson grinned. "That's my special thing," he explained. "Kind of like an artist signing a painting."

"Makes sense." Shannon nodded in agreement.

Growing impatient, Sam Jacobs pushed the conversation back on track. "A couple of kids found a body in a wash a few miles down the road from here. You know or hear anything about that?"

Shannon watched the change come over Benson. Returning the box to the table, he flopped in the chair again. "Nope. Don't know nothing about that. Like I said, I been gone selling stuff. I got names of places that paid me. You can check."

Jacobs wanted to press the guy, but looked to Shannon and saw her shrug her shoulders ever so slightly. He closed the notebook he had been making notes in and shoved it in his pocket. "We may have a few more questions. You planning any more trips soon?"

"Nah," Benson said, obviously relieved that they appeared to be leaving. "I have to build my stock back up."

Jacobs nodded and moved to the open door with Shannon following, both eager for the fresh air beyond.

—

**Three days had elapsed** since the body had been

transported to the Department of Pathology at New Mexico University's Department of Medicine. The deceased was a fish-and-game officer who had disappeared three months earlier. The problem was that he had gone missing north of Ruidoso, nearly two hundred miles from where his remains were found. Despite an unsettling feeling, the visit to Willy Benson had proven unproductive. Without clues, Shannon was trying to make sense of the case by using a spreadsheet posing alternative scenarios and motives. She didn't really need to, as the sheriff's department had competent detectives led by Captain Morales, but it was part of her passion. Unexpectedly, her phone chirped. Concentration broken, she picked up the receiver and was rewarded by a friendly voice.

"Howdy, Shannon. Joel Alvarez here," the Chief Medical Investigator said. "I wanted to talk to you personally about our findings."

"That sounds a bit ominous, sir."

"Oh please, it's just Joel. We're on the same team after all. Anyway, I think you'll find it interesting that our autopsy turned up the murder weapon."

"Really?" She heard the surprise in her own voice.

"I have to admit, it's different. During the preliminary examination, I discovered a chest wound that indicated stabbing as cause of death. Boy, was I wrong. The murder weapon was part of an honest-to-goodness, hand-made arrow. Apache style, I'm told. The arrowhead was attached to a broken wood shaft about three inches long. Straight shot through the left ventricle, then lodged very firmly between two vertebrae. What do you make of that?"

Shannon's mind raced as she mentally arranged pieces of the puzzle. "Joel, do you have that arrowhead?"

"Sure do. I was getting ready to send it to the lab."

"I'll make you a wager that it has two little triangular notches in its base."

Alvarez was bewildered. "How on earth could you possibly know that?"

"Gut feeling."

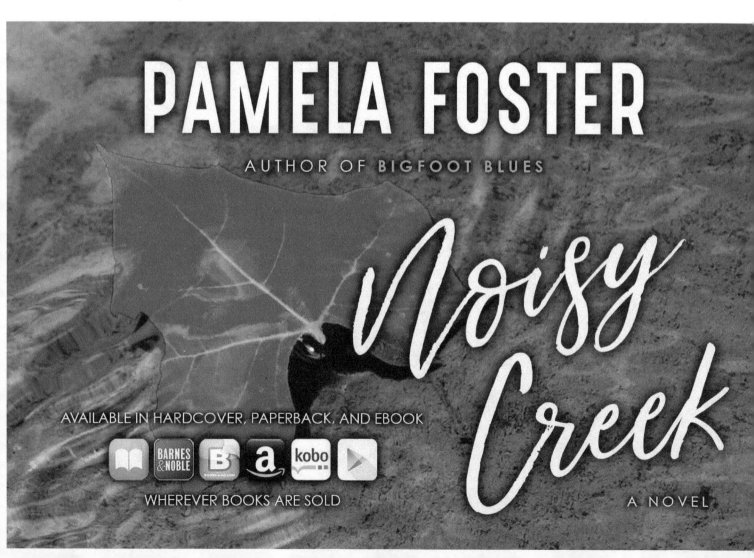

"I could use some of that for six lottery numbers. What are you thinking?"

"I'm thinking I need to thank you, say goodbye, and call the sheriff."

Shannon ended the call and dialed Sheriff Matt Gibson. Gibson listened intently as she related the information from Alvarez and her theory. He had to get to Santa Fe, but knowing her interest in the case, was she comfortable going with Jacobs and Sanchez to finish the affair?

"Tell them I'll meet them at the office."

Jostling once again up the rocky slope, Shannon rode with Sam Jacobs, followed closely by Deputy Tommy Sanchez. Relating her theory and the autopsy findings to the pair before departing, she was pleased they were in agreement.

Arriving at the shabby trailer, they parked in a defensive position, armed with assault rifles. Once more, Sam Jacobs hailed the man inside. From a position of safety behind one of the trucks, Shannon watched as the door grated open in protest and Willy Benson stepped into the open with a pump-action shotgun in hand.

"Willy Benson, you're under arrest for the murder of game officer Phil Watterman. Put the damn shotgun down. Now!"

Benson looked bewildered, but immediately took in the sight of the assault rifles and pushed the shotgun away from him into the dirt.

"Down on your knees and hands on your head," Jacobs barked.

Complying, Benson kneeled and put hands on his head as Sanchez moved forward, covered by Jacobs.

With both shotgun and Benson secured, Sanchez pulled the man to his feet as Jacobs and Shannon walked forward. The three men watched as she moved to the side of the trailer and scooped something from the ground.

Returning to the trio, she held out her palm to reveal a handful of small pink and grey bits of rock—flakes discarded when making arrowheads. With a look of curiosity, Benson's eyes met hers.

"You see, Willy, the devil is in the details. In the end, most criminals are done in by the little things."

# MICHAEL MCLEAN

A native of western Colorado's high country, Michael McLean has packed on horseback in Montana's high country wilderness, mined gold and silver thousands of feet below the earth's surface, fly-fished Yellowstone Park's blue-ribbon waters, and explored the deserts of the West. Through personal and professional experiences he has collected a wealth of information to develop story settings, plots, and characters. His work has been published in *New Mexico Magazine, Rope and Wire,* and *The Penmen Review.* His story "Backroads" was the winner of the 2012 Tony Hillerman Mystery Short Story Contest.

McLean believes the less travelled and often lonely back roads of the West offer intimate access to the land, its people, and their stories. A mining engineer by profession, McLean also has technical publications to his credit. He now works in New Mexico's oil and potash-rich Permian Basin and lives in Carlsbad, New Mexico, with his wife, Sandie. "Little Things" is his first short story to appear in *Saddlebag Dispatches.*

# CHASING ROOSEVELT

*Blake spent three years researching Theodore Roosevelt's time in the Dakota Territory, which included actual hikes and horseback rides over the same land where Roosevelt rode 132 years ago. Unlike other authors who have written about Roosevelt's time in the saddle, he has real-world experience in herding cattle and crossing rivers on horseback.*

## Michael L. Frizell

Michael F. Blake, besides being a fascinating conversationalist, has worked in the film and TV industry for the past 38 years as an Emmy-winning makeup artist. Blake is the author of three books about Lon Chaney. His profiles of the enigmatic silent film actor became the basis for a 2000 documentary for the Turner Classic Movies channel. He has also penned two books on the Western film genre, written several magazine and newspaper articles, and made numerous appearances on documentaries.

*Saddlebag Dispatches* Editor-in-Chief Michael Frizell managed to nail down the busy Blake to discuss his book about *Roosevelt, The Cowboy President: The American West and the Making of Theodore Roosevelt.*

**SD:** *Why did you choose Theodore Roosevelt? What should Western readers know about him?*

**Blake:** I always believe you should write about what you know and what you are interested in. It gives your work a sense of life you don't truly have when writing about something less interesting. I have been a fan of Theodore Roosevelt since I was 8 years-old, and his time in the Dakota territory has been my favorite part. I guess because he was a cowboy, and still being a cowboy-crazy kid at heart, that part of his life always holds a special part of my heart.

In my book, I state that Roosevelt wouldn't be the man on Mount Rushmore, or the man leading the heroic charge up a Cuban hill in the Spanish-American War if it wasn't for his time in the West. He even said he would never have been President if not for his time in the West. The land and the people had a great influence on him. He responded to their ethics, beliefs, and hard work. If he never went hunting buffalo in 1883, I doubt he would have led the conservation fight he did as President. I also believe that the buffalo would likely have been wiped out without his efforts.

Even though he was the first US President born in New York, Theodore was very much a man of the West. He identified with the land and the people. With the exception of Henry Cabot Lodge, his closest friends were from the West and his time in the Dakotas, including Seth Bullock.

By the time Roosevelt left the presidency in 1909, he had set aside over 230 million acres for the

**Blake:** Your word is your bond. That is number one, first and foremost. I love the old cowboy saying that a person is "all hat and no cattle" which means all talk and no action. It is so true. The code is a way of life. You either choose to embrace the meanings or you do not. Same as with the Boy Scouts oath or the Ten Commandments. You have a choice to make it part of your being or not. I believe if you embrace it, you find your life is so much richer and better.

*SD: What do you owe the real people upon whom you base your characters?*

public, including 51 bird sanctuaries, several National Monuments, and created or expanded National Forests. He helped start the Bronx Zoo, and with William Hornaday, they created a project to restore the American buffalo to the Great Plains and elsewhere. They got Congress to set aside 18,000 acres for the American Bison Range in western Montana, which is still doing great work.

Like a true Cowboy, Theodore was a man of his word and lived up to the "riding for the brand" saying 100%.

*SD: You refer to the "Western code of honor" having an influence on Roosevelt in your solicitation. Can you share the code and what it means to you?*

**Blake:** Honesty. Readers can quickly tell if a character is not real or honest. You can make one character a composite of several people, but the main thing is they have to be honest. If they are, then they're real.

*SD: What kind of research do you do, and how long do you spend researching before beginning a book?*

**Blake:** I had been reading about TR for years, so I already kind of knew things. When you're writing about a real person you must know every little detail about them. You may find a slight reference to something in a letter or a comment about a person or incident. That little nugget can often add more detail to the person as a whole.

I am lucky that nowadays a lot of Roosevelt's letters have been digitalized, so it saved me making trips to Harvard University and Washington DC to examine the material firsthand. (It also was a help to the wallet!) One of the positive things in this regard, I did a lot of my research at 1 or 2 in the morning and wasn't restricted by traditional operating hours of archives. For many writers that is a Godsend. Most of us do not get hefty advances if at all, to fund research trips, so material being available via the computer is most helpful. Even when you are writing, you may still be researching. It never really ends until you send your draft to the publisher.

For me, I follow what Louis L'Amour once told me, "You cannot write about the land without seeing and feeling it." And he was so right. I hiked and went by horseback thru the Badlands area in Medora, North Dakota, where Roosevelt's National Park is

located and where he lived. I did this for three years, on and off. I stuck my hands in the bentonite clay when it was wet to feel how damn gooey it becomes when it rains. Now that won't add a lot to the story, but I had a very different view of how hard it was to ride or walk in that stuff. Little thing like that gives you an authoritative voice as a writer and the reader recognizes it right away.

**SD:** *What are the ethics of writing about historical figures?*

**Blake:** Honesty and truth. As a writer, you cannot let your personal feelings or beliefs interfere with the facts. For instance, Roosevelt hunted a great deal. It was part of who he was. Personally, hunting an animal for sport is not something I do. I didn't express my beliefs about this subject, nor did I try to diminish Theodore's passion for it. Instead, I explain to the reader why hunting was so important to Roosevelt with the hope they will understand his actions.

Writers should never try to revise history. It is fine if you have uncovered new facts which rewrite what we were led to believe. If a writer has uncovered something new, their work must have hard evidence to prove it is factual. Anything else is pure conjecture. I prefer to do what Sgt. Joe Friday of *Dragnet* would do, stick to the facts.

Now there are times when you may not have enough facts to explain a situation. In cases like that, you state what facts are available and offer an opinion as to why something happened. I had this situation present itself in my Roosevelt book. There was a story quoted in two books about Theodore's time in the West where he and Bill Merrifield went into a Cheyenne camp and Merrifield challenged them to a shooting contest with rifles, which he claimed he won. Something bothered me about this story. This incident only appears in two books (one published in 1921 and the other in 2011). Merrifield is the source of the story, which he first told after Theodore had died in 1919. It was said that Merrifield had a healthy ego and he once stated that he told Roosevelt to do this or that. Now, I feel I know Roosevelt pretty well. One thing I can tell you is he was not one to boss around!

What made me suspicious of this story was that Roosevelt in all of his writings (he wrote 35 books and hundreds of magazine articles), never *once* mentioned this incident. For Roosevelt, this would have been a big thing, and he certainly would not miss telling this

tale. I went to his diaries for this time period and the only note was "passed an Indian camp." No mention of going to the camp or having a shooting contest. Nothing. In the book, I present the facts that are available and based on them, offer my opinion that this incident never happened. I leave it up to the reader to either agree or disagree.

**SD:** *What was your hardest scene to write?*

**Blake:** His last few years. I wish he never took that damned South American river trip. Trying to save a canoe in the river, he cut his leg and it got infected. He nearly died on that trip. You can see from that point on, the robust man was no longer and his health began to suffer. I always have a hard time writing the demise of a person I have spent a great deal of time studying. I had the same issue when I wrote my Lon Chaney books.

**SD:** *What did you edit out of this book?*

**Blake:** Honestly, only one thing. I had written an appendix that had his first major public speech he gave on July 4, 1886, in Dickinson (North Dakota). While I use some of his speech in the text, I could see it would open a Pandora's box. "How come you only printed that speech and not this one or that one?" So, I cut the appendix.

**SD***: Is there a scene in the book you enjoyed the most?*

**Blake:** Oh, that's an easy answer! There was this fella in the Dakota Territory called Jerry Packard. He was something of a trouble-maker and known to be something of a braggart. Well, he stopped at Roosevelt's Elkhorn ranch one day when Theodore wasn't there (he was hunting). Looking around, he said to Roosevelt's friend, Bill Sewall, that this was a nice ranch and if "Four Eyes" (Roosevelt) wanted it so bad he could fight for it, even with blood.

A couple of days later, Theodore rides up to the cabin from his trip and Sewall tells him what Packard had said. "Is that so?" Theodore replied. He got back on his horse and rode to Packard's cabin, and banged on the door. When Packard answered, Roosevelt, said, "I understand you have threatened to kill me on sight. I have come over to see when you want to begin the killing, and to let you know that, if you have anything to say against me, now is the time for you to say it."

Packard could only stammer out a reply he was misunderstood and misquoted. Ironically, the two men became friends after this incident!

**SD:** *How many hours a day do you write?*

**Blake:** It varies. Now that I am retired, I can write all day—or night—long! I have been known to go six hours without a break. When you are writing about something you either love or are terribly interested in, time can fly. I once started writing the Roosevelt book at 11pm and finished at 6 in the morning! For me it was so much fun writing about this subject, the time just flew.

By the way, I do not believe in writer's block! That is an excuse. Sure, you hit something that isn't working. You just have to go back and re-write it. As long as your hands are on the keys, something will come out. Maybe not what you want, but it is something. You keep at it. Suddenly those keys are dancing again. There is always a solution. Sometimes you have to drop the scene because it wasn't working for the narrative. Or you just need to take a different approach. But you will never find the answer if you whine "Oh, I've got writer's block! Boo-hoo!" It is a lame excuse. Just get back writing.

**SD:** *What was an early experience where you learned that language had power?*

**Blake:** Watching *Gunsmoke* or a John Wayne film as a kid. When Wayne said something you knew it was real. Same with James Arness as Marshal Dillon. No man ever said "Hold it!" with greater authority.

I wasn't a great reader growing up until I got interested in film history at the age of 10. That's when I discovered Kevin Brownlow's great book *The Parade's Gone By.* His knowledge was so great about the silent film era and yet he made everything so conversational and easy to understand. A lot of folks write about cinema (and many don't know what the hell they're talking about!) and they love to use what I call "the $50 words" to impress the reader and colleagues. Between reading all of Brownlow's books and Louis L'Amour, I learned that good storytelling, not $50 words, have the power to move, delight, and educate readers. That is how I approach my books. I want the reader to sit down with my book and it is like I am telling them a story over a cup of coffee in a diner. For me, it is the best way to write.

*The Cowboy President: The American West and the Making of Theodore Roosevel*t reveals how his time spent in the Western Dakota Territory helped him recover from an overwhelming personal loss, but more importantly, how it transformed him into the man etched onto Mount Rushmore, a man who is still rated as one of the top five Presidents in American history. Unlike other Roosevelt biographies, The Cowboy President details how the land, the people, and the Western code of honor had an enormous impact on Theodore and how this experience influenced him in his later years. The book, published by Globe Pequot Press / TwoDot is available now wherever fine paperbacks and ebooks are sold.

—*Michael Frizell is a prolific writer, the editor of* The Learning Assistance Review for the National College Learning Center Association, *and the Director of Student Learning Services at Missouri State University. He and his wife, Julia, a high school English teacher, live in Springfield, Missouri. His new graphic novel,* Bender, *is now available wherever books are sold. He can be reached at* **michael@oghmacreative.com.**

# BAD DAY in BLACK ROCK

A SHORT STORY BY DENNIS DOTY

Levi Sampson plucked the key ring off the desk. He stretched his aching back muscles, then walked back to the jail's single row of cells and unlocked the only one that was occupied.

"You can go on home now, Mister Zack. There's beans and coffee on the stove in the office if you think your stomach can handle 'em."

"Thanks, Levi. I'll pass. I need coffee, but I don't trust yours."

"If you're going by Miss Cindy's cafe, tell her the marshal should be back today or tomorrow. She'll want to know."

"My head feels like I was kicked by a mule. What did I do, anyway?"

Levi chuckled. "You was waving your pistol around threatening to kill Deke Johnson over Miss Celia. Sorry about your head."

"Huh. What did you hit me with?" Zack reached up to feel the side of his head. "Dang! I've got a lump the size of a goose egg."

"Shotgun barrel," Levi said, ducking his head to hide a broad grin.

"From now on, I'll be doing my drinking when the marshal's in town. You're a hard man, Levi." He picked up his battered hat off the bunk, wincing as he plopped it on his head.

"Just trying to do my job. It ain't personal."

"I know it ain't, but Marshal Hendrix would only have cracked me on the jaw with a fist. You and your shotgun left a reminder."

"Don't reckon it'll kill you. You could drink beer, ya know. You're a much nicer drunk when you stay off the whiskey."

"I know. Seems like I get a mad on every time I touch the stuff. I'll have to think some about the beer. Do I get my gun back?"

"Yeah. I don't worry about you when you're sober. Come on out to the office and I'll fetch it for you." Levi led the way to the office and pulled Zack's pistol out of the desk drawer, then handed it to him butt-first.

Zack thumbed the loading gate open and spun the cylinder to check his loads, then shoved it into his holster. "Sorry for the trouble I caused. Be seeing you."

"Take care of yourself, Zack." Levi held the door open and stood watching as Zack walked shakily down the street to the stable.

He leaned against the door jamb, rolling a smoke while his deep brown eyes surveyed the dusty street. A bay and a black were tied in front of the saloon, and a chestnut with one white sock stood hitched at the bank. In front of the general store, was a buckboard with a small woman sitting on the seat. A slight breeze rippled the tops of the cottonwoods along the creek, but gave no respite from the heat to the few citizens who were stirring about below. It was as if nature held her breath, waiting.

*Waiting for what? Whatever it is, I hope I can handle it.*

Zack and Miss Cindy weren't the only ones who would be happy to see Marshal Hendrix return. Levi looked at the unfinished paperwork on the desk. The marshal had been privately teaching him his letters, but he still struggled with keeping the log and reading the wanted posters. Reading and writing intimidated him. Back in Mississippi, it was not only unnecessary to teach a field hand to read, it was illegal.

All that changed when the Army of the Tennes-see swept through. Levi's world upended overnight, but the Jubilee came with a price. Levi and all the other former slaves needed to find a way to make a living in this new world. Many sold themselves back into slavery by becoming sharecroppers on their former plantations.

Levi had known that he would never be free in Mississippi, so he came west. He crossed the Red River and took a job dragging longhorns out of the Big Thicket down in Texas, where he learned to ride and rope. He tried learning to shoot, as well, but his skill with a pistol was never more than passable. When they had gathered a herd of six-hundred head or so, Mister Johnson asked him to come along on the drive to Ellsworth. It was three months of the hardest and most dangerous work he'd ever done, but they arrived in Ellsworth with five hundred and forty-seven head. Levi drew his pay and turned west. He never looked back.

Like so many men uprooted by the war, Levi drift-

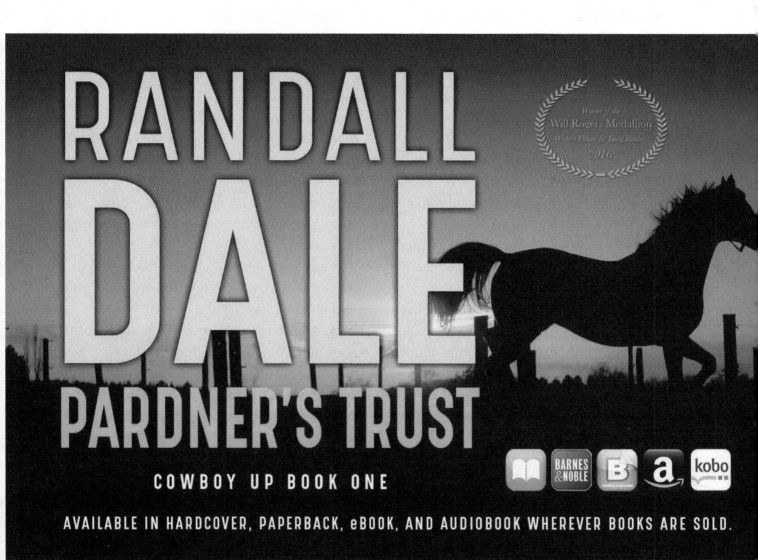

ed from town to town taking work when he could find it, going hungry when he couldn't. He worked cattle, plowed fields, mucked out stables, and emptied spittoons. Many of the cowboys he met scoffed at work they couldn't do from a saddle, but Levi figured, if it was honest work, it was worth being proud of. If it came with a meal and a coin, he gave it his best. Sometimes he had to ride the grub-line, but he always managed to chop some wood, sharpen an axe, or muck a stall before he rode on.

When he arrived in Black Rock, he asked around for work and was surprised when Marshal Hendrix said he needed a deputy.

"I don't know about telling no white man what to do." Levi had knotted his brow in deep thought.

"Son, out here, a man can be whatever he wants to be, so long as he has the will."

Marshal Hendrix had looked hard at Levi and offered his hand. Levi shook it and pinned on a badge. To his surprise, he quickly found that most of the town's citizens seemed to like him, and he liked them.

It was a whole new experience for him, and more than a little disconcerting.

So, he leaned against the doorjamb to the marshal's office, surveying the street and wishing Hendrix hadn't been called away to Denver.

Old Man Jameson sat in his usual rocker in front of the hotel. As far as Levi knew, only he and Marshal Hendrix knew the story about that old man. He remembered his surprise when the marshal had told him Jameson had served as a major under Mosby in the war. After the war, he'd ramrodded a West Texas ranch known for their rough and tumble crew, then served for five years as a deputy marshal in Abilene. He might look harmless, but Levi knew there was a Colt under his left arm in a shoulder rig and a pepper-box in his right coat pocket. He was an expert with both. Levi smiled as he thought how surprised the citizens of the town would be to know all that.

Levi ran a hand through his wooly hair. Might as well take a turn about town then stop in at Wallace's and get it cut. Stepping back inside, he put on his hat,

crossed the room, and took a double-barreled Greener out of the rack. He knew his limitations with a pistol, and the Greener had an intimidation value that couldn't be beat. Most men would back down from a shotgun, especially at close range. That knowledge had come in handy more than once in the six years he'd worn the badge.

He walked the boards down to the hotel with the shotgun tucked under his arm. Pausing to put out his smoke, he nodded. "You doing alright today, Mister Jameson?"

"Just fine, Levi. You?"

"I could do with some rain or a breeze, but other than that, I'm good, sir."

"It sure is quiet today." Jameson squinted up at Levi, a questioning look on his face.

"I noticed. Almost too quiet." Levi glanced uneasily at the peaceful street.

"My thoughts exactly. You keep your eyes peeled, you hear?"

"Oh, that I will, Mister Jameson. I don't know exactly why, but I'm glad you're out here today."

"You don't worry about this end of things, son. I'm loaded for bear."

Levi chuckled. "Aren't you always?"

"Well, now that you mention it." Jameson offered a rare wry smile and spat a stream of tobacco juice into the street. He plucked the stick and his knife from his lap and began adding to the wood shavings at his feet.

Levi pulled his hat brim down slightly and ambled across the street to the store. He recognized the woman on the wagon now.

"Howdy there, Missus Adams. Clay picking up supplies inside?"

"That's right, Marshal."

"Now, Missus Adams, you knows I'm only a deputy. You don't need to be sitting out here in the hot sun. You ought to go inside where it's cooler."

"Don't worry about me. I'll be fine, thank you. Clay should be along any minute."

"Yes, ma'am. Whatever you say." Levi caught a movement out of the corner of his eye and turned to look toward the blacksmith and stables.

Four hard-looking men were walking their horses down the dusty street. Levi's scalp tingled. What was it about them that set his nerves on edge? Then he noticed it—their horses were better than the average drifting cowboy could afford. Much better.

*Lord, I wish the marshal was here. I hope I'm ready for this.* He stood with his hand on the sideboard of the wagon bed and watched them. When they passed his office, one of them, the scarecrow-looking fellow on the right, peeled off and turned into the alley.

Levi looked across the street, all doubt about their intentions gone. Jameson had seen them, too, and nodded slightly to Levi. Two of the men stopped in front of the bank and looked around before dismounting and looping their horse's reins over the rail, without tying them. A slightly paunchy fellow with a patch over his left eye and a skinny freckle-faced kid went into the bank. The kid looked nervous, and Levi hoped he wouldn't do anything foolish in there. Not that he could do anything about it.

The fourth rider continued down the street. Levi forced a friendly smile and nod as the man passed. He looked to be Mexican or maybe Indian, with a long hawk's beak of a nose stuck in the middle of his swarthy face. He ignored the smile and nod.

Just then, Clay came out of the store and walked up to the wagon. "Sorry it took so long, Em." He rolled a heavy sack of flour off his shoulder and placed it and a small bag in the wagon bed. "Howdy, Levi."

"Clay." Levi kept his voice low and even. "Git Miz Emma into the store—and take your rifle with you." Levi didn't look at him. Instead, he caught Jameson's eye and tilted his head slightly towards the man who had ridden past. Jameson gave a single nod, rose, folding his pocket knife, and ambled casually to the doorway of the hotel where he turned and faced the street.

"What's going on, Levi?"

"Not now, Clay. Just do as I asked of you."

Emma was already climbing down from the wagon. Clay helped her down and reached across grabbing a Winchester from under the footboard.

"Clay, keep an eye on the alley by my office," Levi said as Emma entered the store. He moved on down the boards toward the saloon across from the bank. He stopped at the batwings and glanced inside before entering. Two cowboys sat at a table, playing cards and drinking quietly. Sam, the baldheaded saloon

# "LET'S SADDLE UP A COUPLE OF THESE CRITTERS AND GET FORKED."

– Rawhide Robinson

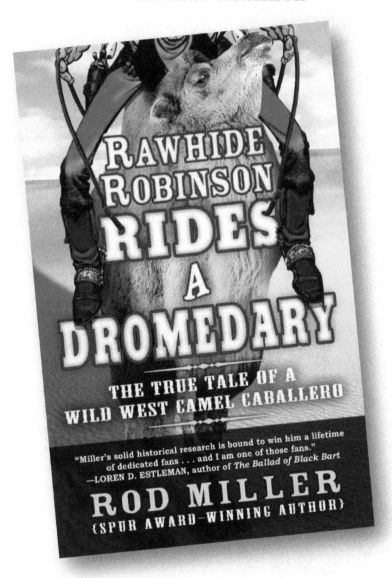

Rawhide Robinson wants no part of camels. But, as our ordinary cowboy always does when he finds himself in the midst of extraordinary events, he rises to the occasion. Ride the waves with Rawhide Robinson as he visits exotic ports of call acquiring camels for the US Army. Page-turning excitement, heart-pounding adventures, and smile-stimulating tall tales are yours to enjoy when cowboy meets camel in the latest Rawhide Robinson novel from writer Rod Miller.

**Rawhide Robinson Rides a Dromedary | Five Star | ISBN 978-1-4328-3729-7**

www.RawhideRobinson.com

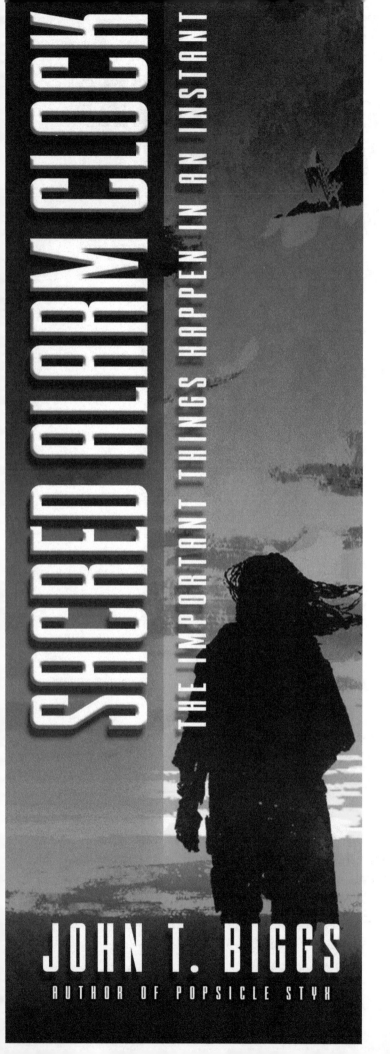

**SACRED ALARM CLOCK**

**THE IMPORTANT THINGS HAPPEN IN AN INSTANT**

**JOHN T. BIGGS**

**AUTHOR OF POPSICLE STYX**

keeper, was polishing glasses with a greasy rag. Levi stepped inside and turned back to watch the street over the batwings.

"Trouble, Levi?" Sam hadn't missed his unusual movement. Levi suppressed a nervous smile. Sam didn't miss much.

"Nothing I can't handle, Sam. Just keep your head down for a bit." Levi heard some scurrying behind him and assumed that the cowboys and Sam were taking cover.

"Wal, lookit what we got here." The shorter of the two cowboys drawled. "We got us a ni—" He cut off what he was about to say when Levi turned to face him and flipped his vest back to show the badge.

"Shut up, Will." His companion seemed to have more sense. "Sorry 'bout that, Marshal. We aren't looking for trouble."

"And we ain't having no trouble in here." Sam laid his shotgun on the bar, carelessly pointed at the two card players.

"No, sir. We don't want no trouble. None, at all." The level-headed cowboy gave his companion a hard stare.

Levi turned back toward the street, knowing that Sam had his back. He gauged the distance to the horses across the street. Forty feet, give or take. Well within the range of his shotgun. He glanced to his left. The scarecrow-looking fellow had come out of the alley and stood leaning against the corner of the building. Levi noted the tied-down gun and the rifle he held close against his leg.

Glancing to his right, he noticed that the hawk-faced man hadn't dismounted, but had turned his horse at the end of the street and sat leaning forward with his forearm on the saddle horn while his horse danced skittishly, hooves making little puffs of dust in the street.

The door to the bank opened and Red came out with his hand on his pistol butt. Behind him, Eye Patch backed out the door with his gun drawn, a heavy-looking flour sack in his left hand. Quickly scanning the street and seeing nothing amiss, they flicked their reins over the horses' heads and started to mount.

Levi took a deep breath and sent a silent prayer to heaven. He stepped through the batwings with the shotgun leveled at the two men. As their feet touched the stirrups, his challenge rang out, "That's far enough, boys. Drop your guns."

Both men looked to the sound of Levi's voice. Eye Patch froze where he was, but Red tried to bring his gun to bear. He was much too slow, and Levi's blast knocked him out of the saddle to sprawl over the hitching rail. Red's horse screamed and pitched a bucking fit over the stray shotgun pellets that had hit his ear and rump.

For Levi, time seemed to expand and every beat of his pounding heart seemed like a full minute. Everything seemed to happen at once.

Eye Patch ducked behind the bucking horse and snapped a shot at Levi. Another shot rang out from Levi's right and was answered from the hotel doorway as the bullet from his right tore past Levi's head and buried itself in the saloon's front wall. Eye Patch's shot went wide and shattered the saloon window before plowing to a stop in the bar.

With no clear shot at Eye Patch, Levi dove back through the batwings and rolled to his feet. Another pair of shots were fired, one from Eye Patch, which missed, the other was a rifle barking from the mercantile down the street. Levi heard a grunt off to his left, indicating someone was hit, followed by a scream that made the hair on the back of his neck stand up.

"Don't shoot! I give up." Eye Patch punctuated his call by throwing his pistol out in the middle of the street.

Levi stepped back through the batwings, his shotgun leveled and his pulse racing. "Git your hands up and walk out here where I can see you."

Eye Patch walked slowly into the street with his hands raised. Levi noted his empty holster before risking a glance to his left. Scarecrow lay writhing in the street with something sticking out of a wound in his shoulder, and was calling for someone to help him. His pistol was still in his holster and his rifle lay ten feet away with a shattered stock.

Levi looked right and saw Hawk Face sprawled lifeless in the street. His horse was nowhere in sight. He turned back to Eye Patch.

"Git on your knees," he said, his usually friendly baritone now a gravelly growl. Eye Patch didn't protest, dropping to his knees.

"Easy, Levi," said a voice from behind him, and ice shot through his veins. "Are you okay? You're shaking like you was shot," said the voice, which he recognized as Joe's.

"I'm okay, Joe. I just never killed a man before."

"He played his hand, Levi. Take a deep breath now."

Levi realized that he'd been holding his breath and took a moment to exhale. He drew several deep breaths before he stepped out to pick up the pistol Eye Patch had tossed.

"All right, get up. Jail's down there to your right."

Levi marched Eye Patch down to his wounded companion and told him to halt. He glanced at the wounded man. Four inches of polished rifle stock stuck out from a ragged wound in his shoulder. Clay's bullet had struck the stock of his rifle as he was about to fire at Levi. Probably saved his life.

As Doc Walker ran up to check on the wounded man, Levi asked, "You got him, Doc?"

"Yeah, Levi. He won't be no trouble, and if he is, I'll finish him off." Doc patted his holster with a nod.

Levi took the wounded man's pistol and tucked it behind his belt, then picked up the busted rifle. He marched his prisoner down to the jail and locked him in the same cell Zack had occupied.

"You want to give me your name or do I have to go through my dodgers to find it?"

"Simms, Marshal. It's Simms."

"Buck Simms, of the Simms gang?"

"That's right. So, what's next?"

"You all sure had a bad day in Black Rock. Well, Simms, we've got a circuit judge here. He'll be around in a week or two and you'll get a fair trial. Then, we'll likely ship you off to Denver to face charges there. You boys are wanted for murder up that way. Likely, they'll hang you."

"How'd you know we were coming?"

A SHORT STORY BY THE AUTHOR OF *STONEWALL*

# JOHN J. DWYER

## RIDING THE SHORTGRASS COUNTRY

"I didn't. Your horses gave you away."

"Horses? How's that?"

"No drifting cowboy can afford horses like those. So, why Black Rock?"

"We ran into your marshal up the trail a bit. We planned to rob him, but after we shot him, we found some papers that said who he was. We figured that a town without a marshal would be easy pickin's."

"Your mistake. How far up the trail is the marshal?" The drumming in Levi's chest grew intense again.

"Not more than an hour or two, but the buzzards have got him by now. He had three bullets in him."

Still carrying his shotgun, Levi rushed out of the office and ran down the street. "Clay, I need to borrow your buckboard. Take Em over to the hotel. I don't know how soon I'll be back. Tell Clyde I'm paying."

"Do you need someone to go with you?"

"No, but after you get Miz Em settled, tell Doc I'm hoping to be bringing him another patient. Marshal Hendrix has been shot."

"I'll do it. Don't you worry."

Levi climbed up on the seat and turned the wagon around. It was all he could do to hold the horses to a trot while his whole being wanted to gallop to Marshal Hendrix.

—

**Three hours later**, **night** had fallen on Black Rock when a buckboard came bouncing behind a pair of racing, foam-flecked horses. It stopped in front of Doc's office and Levi leapt down from the seat, calling for the doctor.

Doc Walker took one quick look at Marshal Hendrix. "Let's get him inside."

Levi helped Doc slide him out of the buckboard, then they carried him inside and placed him on the examination table.

"Good thing you had Tom let me know you were bringing him. Now get outta here and let me work."

"I'll be right outside, Doc." *Lord, don't takes him now. I needs him here.* Levi wondered at his discovery of how close he had become to Marshal Hendrix. *He's my friend.* He realized that he had never had a friend before.

He stepped outside the office and hailed Tommy O'Brien, who was passing by. "Tommy. Come here, quick." He waved.

Tommy trotted across the street. "What is it, Mister Sampson?"

"Tommy, Marshal Hendrix has been shot. I've got to stay here with him. Will you walk Clay Adams' team cool, take 'em to the stable, unhitch the buckboard, and fork 'em some hay? I'll pay you four-bits." He dug in his pants pocket for some change.

"Aw, heck, you don't have to pay me for that. Marshal Hendrix is a friend of mine."

Levi smiled and pressed the coins into Tommy's hand anyway. Going back inside, he paced outside the surgery door, pausing from time to time to send a silent prayer.

The front door opened, and Miss Cyndy came in carrying a covered basket that smelled powerfully of fried chicken and baked beans.

"How is he, Levi?" Her lip trembled with emotion.

"I don't really know, Miss Cindy. The doc's working on him. He chased me out here."

"I'll wait with you."

"That'll be fine, ma'am. I don't think Doc's gonna let him eat for a while though."

"Oh," she started as she remembered her basket. "This isn't for him." She set the basket on a sideboard. "I thought you might be hungry. You've had a busy day."

"Yes, ma'am. Thank you, ma'am."

"Levi, you don't have to call me ma'am. You know my name." Her soft words were the first soothing thing Levi had heard all day.

"Yes, ma'—Miss Cindy." Levi pulled a chair across to the sideboard and uncovered the basket. He removed a steaming plate of fried chicken and beans. Looking surprised, he pulled out a bottle of whiskey and looked at Miss Cindy, one eyebrow raised.

She said nothing but stalked off into Doc's private quarters. In a moment or two, she returned with two glasses and set them on the sideboard.

"Pour one for me, too, Levi. I think I could use it."

Levi poured two stiff drinks and watched as Cindy tossed hers down like a Texas cowhand at the end of the drive. He held the bottle over her empty glass and looked at her. His eyes asked the question.

"Please. One more."

Levi poured then set the bottle down and dug into the chicken. He hadn't realized how hungry he was. They sipped their whiskey as Levi ate.

"Thank you, Miss Cindy. That sure did hit the spot." Levi tossed off the last sip of his whiskey, stood and resumed his pacing. He had barely crossed the room when the surgery door opened and Doc stepped out, closing it softly behind him.

"How is he, Doc? Did Levi get him here in time?"

"He's going to pull through. He's resting now. I took three bullets out of him. One nicked his liver, and he lost a lot of blood. I stopped the bleeding and repaired the damage. Another was in his shoulder, but didn't do any real damage. He'll have a sore wing for a while."

"You said three, Doc." Cindy skewered him with a look, demanding the full report.

"Cindy, I'm sorry. The third bullet was in his thigh. It broke his femur bone. I took the bullet out and stopped the blood. He has a good splint on it."

"But...."

"But I'm afraid he's going to have a long road ahead. When he gets his strength back, he'll have to learn to walk again, if he can, and he's going to have a bad limp when he does. The bone was seriously fractured. I removed all the bone splinters I could find, and the bone will eventually knit itself, but that leg will be shorter and painful to walk on."

"As soon as you can, Doc, I want him moved to my place in back of the diner, where I can keep an eye on him." She paused, then asked so softly it was almost a whisper, "Can I see him?"

"Go on in, but try not to wake him. Rest is the best thing for him now."

Cindy hurried to the door, took a deep breath, squared her shoulders, then stepped in and closed the door behind her.

"You can go in too, Levi."

"Is you blind, Doc?"

"What? What do you mean by that?"

"She's in love with him, Doc. They're going to need some alone time."

"Well, I'll be damned."

"Likely we both will, but in the meanwhile, how about a drink?" He held up the bottle Cindy had brought.

"A welcome thought, Levi, certainly."

"How long you gonna keep him here, Doc?"

"He can go home in a day or so when he's comfortable with using crutches, but he's going to need someone to stay with him and lend a hand. I guess Cindy can handle that. You in a hurry to get him home?"

"I'm thinking that the food and service at the diner might be kinda poor until he gets outta here."

Doc chuckled. "You may be right about that." He lifted the glass that Cindy had previously used. "To a speedy recovery, then."

"God help the hungry." Levi smiled for the first time that day as they tossed off their drinks.

A while later, Levi peeked in on the marshal and Cindy. She was sitting in a chair next to his bed, holding his hand next to her heart, and had fallen asleep. Levi backed out and closed the door softly behind him.

Leaving Doc's office, Levi took a turn about the town. Assured that all was well, he stopped at the mayor's house and knocked. The mayor's wife answered the door. "Oh, Levi. It's so good to see you. Won't you come in?"

"Thank you kindly, ma'am." Levi removed his hat as he entered and waited while she went upstairs to fetch the mayor.

"Ah, Levi. I heard about Marshal Hendrix. How's he doing?"

Levi filled him in on what the doctor had said and the prognosis. "I thought you'd want to know, Mister Mayor. Marshal Hendrix doesn't know it yet, but I thought to give you a warning. You're gonna have to start looking for a new marshal."

"Oh, I don't think so, Levi. I'm pretty sure I've got a good one." The mayor's eyes twinkled. "But you might start thinking about who you'd want for a deputy."

# DENNIS DOTY

Dennis Doty, a Southern California native, has been writing fiction since 2004. His stories spring from a vivid imagination, but many have a basis in his many life experiences, including growing up in a small town, the decade he served in the Marine Corps, and stories from two years riding on the old Southwest RCA rodeo circuit.

Dennis presently lives in Appalachia, with his wife and their two dogs, where he divides his time between writing, swapping lies with the other old timers, and yelling at kids to get off his lawn.

After submitting his first short story, "White Buffalo Woman" to appear in the Spring, 2017 issue of *Saddlebag Dispatches*, Dennis so impressed Publisher Dusty Richards that The Ranch Boss invited him to join the magazine staff on a permanent basis. He now serves as Managing Editor, and as Deputy Publishing Director of Galway Press's parent company, Oghma Creative Media.

Dennis blogs on a regular basis on a multitude of subjects, not the least of which is quality in editing. You can learn more about Dennis and his writing at **www.dennisdotywebsite.com**

# LEARNIN' HOW TO COWBOY UP

*My dad could "cowboy up" with the best of them. I used to love listening to his stories when I was a boy, thinking maybe someday I could be a cowboy, too.*

*George Gilland*

My dad could "cowboy up" with the best of them. I used to love listening to his stories when I was a boy, thinking maybe someday I could be a cowboy, too.

When I was four years old, Dad moved the family and all our gear a good 75 miles from Shields, North Dakota by team and wagon to our new ranch on the Standing Rock Sioux Reservation, a little over 20 miles south of Thunder Hawk, South Dakota and about a hundred miles from the Indian Agency at Fort Yates, North Dakota. Our nearest neighbors were eight miles by road from our ranch and we didn't have a car or truck during the first years. That happened to be back in 1946, and in many ways, it was more like 1846 – no electricity, no phone, no running water, no automobiles, and not much in the way of roads. Dad's mother's people were Lakota and his father had settled in the area when it was still Dakota Territory. Between them, they knew the country west of the Missouri River pretty well.

Our ranch was made up of 320 acres Dad had bought plus another three sections of Sioux tribal land that we leased. When we arrived, there weren't any buildings and not much of the land was fenced. We lived in an old army tent most of the first sum-

mer. It was big for a tent, I think about 12 feet wide and 24 feet long. Dad even hauled in some hardpan dirt, wet it down, and packed it for a floor. Mother would sweep that floor every day. I never quite figured out why she would sweep a dirt floor.

Dad had to put in a lot of fencing right away for

the 40 head of Herefords and the horses we started out with. He bought an old homesteader shack for us to live in, but it had to be moved to our land. By fall Dad managed to get the house moved to our place hauling it the two-mile distance with two teams and two wagons. It took several days and quite a bit of jacking to get that house high enough to get the wagons under it. He put a long pole on each wagons running gear, then the house on the poles, and pulled the wagons with horses. The trail crossed a dry creek where it was too narrow for the wagons and the house, so Dad and my oldest brother Bob did the hard work of shoveling the banks down to widen them.

When the house was in place, he added a room that went up against a bank and dug a storm cellar. I thought it was kinda neat that we could go from the house to the cellar. Mother was deathly scared of bad storms so she really appreciated the cellar. It seemed like we were all ushered to the cellar every time a cloud drifted by. She had been in a bad storm in her childhood and people had died, so I suppose her fears were justified.

We never had a lot of money, and I can't remember a time when we didn't have some chores to do. I didn't know any other life so it wasn't so bad. All eight of us kids growing up on the ranch spent our time mostly taking care of the cows and horses. My oldest brother Bob was 12 years older than me, and I was number five, so there was plenty of us for company. With 20 or more horses around, we never were short of something to ride, but some of those horses made me sit up and ride to stay with them. Out of necessity, I learned to ride some bouncy horses. Dad liked his saddle horse to be at least 1,200 pounds and grain fed. When he was young, he had to ride long distances all day, and he said small horses would play out and you would be walking before the day was done. "Quarter horses are too small for working cattle in this country—they are built like bulldogs with no withers and too low in the front. If you had to rope something, the saddle would likely pull right over its head," he'd say.

We finally got a car in 1947—a 1936 Chevrolet that Dad had traded for some cash and 300 ash fence posts with Ed Ebert. The Ebert place was about 12 miles north of ours, and Dad and my brother Bob cut and hauled a lot of posts up there before we got the car. It was a good car, but it wasn't too good in mud.  Once we got stuck on the Athboy Road about 20 miles from home right near Ed and Betty White's place. I thought it was so funny that you could step right off the running board on to the road, but Dad didn't seem to see the humor in it! Ed White came and pulled the car off the road, then he took Dad and us boys to our home in his Jeep, but he didn't use the road, rather he just followed the ridges and hills most of the time. It was a scenic ride.  He came back about three days later and got Dad so he could retrieve our car plus Mother and my sisters, who had stayed on with Ed's wife Betty until the road dried up.

Dakota weather can be pretty harsh and unpredictable.  The nearest school was eight miles away and getting there sometimes was a problem, especially in the winter.  One year Dad rented a place that was only a couple of miles from the school so the older kids could get there.  During the winter of 1949-50, Dad moved a little house over by the school so we could get to school—good thing, too, because that was one hard winter.  Bob didn't have to go to school anymore so he stayed home and took care of our cattle and horses, while Dad went over to help our neighbors, Herb and Tom Lyman, with feeding their cattle.  They had several hundred cows, and they kept their calves too and ran them until they were yearlings.  Tom fed the calves, and Herb and Dad fed the cows by pitchfork, with teams and hay racks. When the snow got deep, they put the hay racks on sled runners. Dad said that they worked from early morning until late at night just to get enough hay out for the cows.

We didn't get around much that winter because the snow was higher than most fence posts and the roads were blocked until spring. Then one day we heard the sound of two Cats equipped with snow plows coming down the road making a trail.  In snow that deep, I couldn't see the Cats but I could hear their roar and clatter and see the snow breaking and pile up to the side as they came along. That was a hard winter and many ranchers lost a lot of their cattle. We didn't lose our cattle, but the Lyman family lost a bunch. That spring when the ice went out on the river, all of us from school went down to the Grand River to have a look. The river was way out of its banks—in

Dad contended that it was safer for us kids to ride bareback so if we fell off we couldn't get hung up in the stirrups. Until I was ten or so I rode bareback, which is not what it's cracked up to be, although it is warmer in winter than being up on a saddle, in summer horses sweat, too. Bouncing along on a sweaty

places it was more than a half-mile wide. Big cakes of ice were a floating along and we saw dead cows on top of some of the ice cakes—it was not a pretty sight!

Despite the hard years, Dad loved the life on the ranch—that he was a jack of all trades and could mend and fix things probably helped. Sometimes, he did have a way at minimizing the negative parts of being a cowboy, but even though he taught us all he could about cowboying, he wasn't so sure it would be the best life to follow for all his kids. Others in my life, besides Dad, did encourage me to be a cowboy. Among them was my Dad's brother, my Uncle Jim, who put me on his saddle horse in the corral at his place when I was around five. He had ridden home fast and his horse needed to be cooled down so he had me ride him on a walk around the corral for a good while. Riding in that saddle on Uncle Jim's horse was the first time in a saddle for me.

horse tends to cause some rubbing on the legs, mostly on the inside of the knees. After a few miles, your legs get somewhat raw sore then the salt from horse sweat really stings. Still, like my older brothers and sisters, I would rather ride a horse than be around the house. There was always a fence that needed mending or a cow, bull, or a yearling was missing from our bunch so two or more of us got sent out on horses to fix the fence or find the strayed cattle.

Dad told us to always take a jug of water with us when we went riding in the summer, but ever try carrying a jug of water on a horse bareback? He also said if we ran out of the water to look for a spring. We mostly relied on finding a spring, but sometimes we spent more time looking for water than we did cows. Even the water in a stock dam tasted dang good on a blisteringly-hot day miles from home. It could be a little muddy but it was as wet as any other water.

None of us ever did get sick from drinking pasture water either—we guessed it was "pasteurized."

When my oldest sister Betty got married to Nick Tribe, Dad helped them lease some land just across the road from our place and get some cattle. They ran their cattle in common during the summer with Herb

Cows could put a little scare in me, too. When I was around 10, I helped Nick with pulling a calf from one of his heifers. He had a few Herefords with horns and this heifer's horns looked especially sharp. When we had gotten the calf pulled and let the heifer have slack in the rope, she right away took to licking on

GEORGE GILLAND WALKS THE LAND ON HIS RANCH ON THE STANDING ROCK SIOUX RESERVATION, A LITTLE OVER 20 MILES SOUTH OF THUNDER HAWK, SOUTH DAKOTA.

and Tom Lyman. Nick seemed to latch on to me to help him with gathering his cattle, and he had me stay with Betty during the day because he did quite a bit of day work for neighbors and was away a lot. They had a milk cow that I would get in for Betty to milk or for Nick to milk when he got home. Betty was about always expecting (I think they had four kids within about five years), so I often stayed with Betty until Nick would get home. Most days by the time I hot-footed it for home, it was usually after dark. There was a creek in between their place and home that I had to cross. Several times when I was crossing the creek I heard a mountain lion let out a scream. Most times I had to stop and open a wire gate across the road, but when I heard that ol' lion, I could jump right over that gate. It didn't take me long to run on home, either I outran that ole cat or it wasn't hungry!

her calf. Then Nick told me to slip up alongside her and grab the rope off her neck. It seemed simple enough, but about the time I touched the rope by her neck that heifer turned on me and bellowed and ran right at me, blowing snot. I didn't wait for her to bunt me. I thought she was looking for tracks and I decided in a fast hurry to leave her some. I took a run for the corral fence with that heifer right on my rear so close I could feel the hot air hitting on my backside. She didn't run fast enough to catch me though. My hand nicked the top plank on the corral as I went over it, and that plank was at least five feet off the ground. That was a pretty good jump for a kid! Times like that got me to wondering if that brother-in-law really cared much for me.

I had another Uncle Jim—my Mother's brother Jim Williamson—who asked my dad if he would let me

# SHORTGRASS

## JOHN J.
# DWYER

WWW.JOHNJDWYER.COM

ride a pony for him when I was about seven. Uncle Jim had bought a pony for his little kids and he wanted me to ride her to make sure she would be safe for his little ones. Dad said it would be fine with him if I wanted to do it. Sure I would do that. I had ridden some but just old broke horses, and none that bucked, so I hadn't felt the bucked off feeling. I fell off old Corker once or rather was pulled off. I gave my little sister a ride behind me and when we got to trotting she started bouncing and laughing and bounced right over sideways, and pulled me off too. That ended me giving her a ride behind me. Uncle Jim's horse was called Nancy and she was a pretty little pony, a tad bigger than a Shetland. She was supposed to be green broke, but Dad said he thought she had never been riding. If she had, she sure wasn't taught anything, but he told me to just go slow with her and to remember that the two things that got a horse to buck were being scared and being hurt. So avoid them two things. If she wanted

to buck anyway, then she probably had been spoiled by someone previous. If that were the case, then just put on spurs and carry a quirt, and if you were a good enough cowboy to scratch and quirt her till she quit bucking, she would never again buck with you.

I started getting on and off Nancy in the stall, then out in the corral, then got a bridle with a snaffle bit fitted on her. She was easy to jump on bareback and

she went well for me. I think I rode her in the corral for over a month and she would gallop and stop and turn. I wanted to ride her out of the corral, but Dad just said he didn't trust that Nancy horse and thought my older brother should try riding her outside first. They saddled her up. Dad led Nancy, Bob got on, and I opened the corral gate for them, but Nancy acted like a different horse. I think it may have been the saddle or that my brother was a stranger to her, and that snubbing seemed to irritate her too. They managed to get almost ten feet out of the corral gate before Nancy really blew up. She bogged her head and did some good job of bucking, even with Dad snubbing her. He had her snubbed short too, but she still had Bob hanging on with both hands. After a little Dad got her pulled up and stopped with her head up over his knee. My brother was quick to hop right off. Dad wouldn't let me ride Nancy after that, but I still think I would have gotten along with her because she liked me. I think they just scared her but Dad could read horses well and he promptly took Nancy back over to my uncle's. Then he told him that she was just a spoiled horse and to get rid of her before she hurt someone—she sure was no horse for his little kids to be riding.

THE **GILLAND** FAMILY, CIRCA 1938, A FEW YEARS BEFORE THEIR MOVE TO SOUTH DAKOTA.

My mother's family claimed to be from Iowa, but Dad said once that he thought that they must have come from Missouri because they never listened to good advice and always had that "show-me" attitude. Uncle Jim was a good example of that. He not only didn't take Dad's advice and he decided to ride Nancy himself, which landed him in the hospital. Nancy threw both him and the saddle over her head and kicked Uncle Jim as he went to the ground and about tore his jaw off. Uncle Jim did part with Nancy shortly after that, but he had bought another green-broke steel grey mare called Dolly and he had ridden her a little with the help of a good cowboy, Leo Anderson. Leo had taken on the job of riding that Dolly horse while Uncle Jim was getting healed up. Uncle Jim was not a horseman, he was a farmer, and teaching a horse was out of his line of expertise. He was still some sore in the mouth when he came over and took me home with him to give Dolly a ride. She was only 13 or 14 hands, so Leo didn't care to ride her much as he was a tall fellow and weighed somewhere near 200 pounds. I suppose he felt foolish on a little horse, but he said he thought she would play out on him if he rode her a long ride. Somehow I was unanimously selected for that job.

Uncle Jim, Tom Lyman, and Leo were going to work cattle over at neighbor George Minges' place about five miles to the southwest. For a three-year-old, Dolly acted broke enough. It was a cold morning, frosty enough to bring out the buck in a horse if they had one of them. Leo helped me adjust the saddle and I mounted up to give her a walk around the corral—in case she threw me off, it would be easier to catch her again. She was fine, even neck reined. Leo had done well with her. About the time I got around the corral, out of the barn came Tom with his horse Scotty, a light sorrel gelding with a little white on his face and a couple of white socks. Tom just swings up into the saddle like he was in a hurry, and Scotty quickly bogged his head and went to bucking. Around the corral, they went and out the gate by the barn into the

hay yard. The gate was latched but Scotty hit it with enough force that it popped open. It was dark yet, the barn had a light out front, but there was no light out in the hay yard. You couldn't see that horse buck but you could hear the commotion though and Scotty was just a squealing. After a few minutes, Tom came riding his mount back into the corral like nothing had happened and we headed for the Minges place. Dolly went just fine. She did pause at the river, but I think she didn't know what it was. She had to stick her nose down and smell the river—maybe she had x-ray vision and looked to see how deep it was—but then she went right across. It was only about three feet deep, but in the dark, it spooked me a little too. It was a great day for me. Leo was a lot of help and I had a lot of encouragement from about everyone there.

Oscar Weisinger was another fellow I met at the Minges ranch. He was always doing something to get a laugh, but he was a good hand who really knew his stuff about working cattle. Leo said that Oscar was George Minges' right-hand man but that he was Tom Lyman's, right-hand man. They showed me how to flank a calf and flip it on the ground, and how to bulldog a calf by grabbing it around the neck with one arm and catching its nose and an ear. Then we would "pig-tie" the calf by slipping a rope around one front leg and wrapping the two hind legs to the front leg, wrap it a few times, then make a half-hitch by bringing the rope end back under the loop. It was lots of fun and there were plenty of calves to practice on. Some of them were big and husky, but even the little ones were a handful for me. One took off just as I got my arm around its neck and rubbed my face right against the plank corral giving me a few slivers and a red cheek. I had a lot of encouragement from the hands, even George Minges said, "Hang with him, cowboy." I managed to get that calf flipped, after a fashion, and I received a couple of kicks—calves can kick in a fast hurry when you get too close or grab them. I began to look forward to getting done with the calf branding a long while before we were done. I hadn't eaten enough lunch either and I worked up an ambitious appetite. Riding back to Lyman's place I was tired, dirty, hungry, and sore in many places. I had never before put in such a long day. We had ridden out in the dark and rode home in the dark. I guess it was a pretty long day for a boy.

Dad always rode like he was in an endurance race. He could ride across the country over to a neighbor's to help and never be late getting there. He would ride his horse on a gut-jarring trot all the way, periodically he would lope out his horse for a few hundred yards, then right back to a hard trot again. Jake Wiener, whose place was about nine miles southwest of our place, had a bunch of mules, some were Jacks that were not cut, and they all needed to be branded, ranging from yearlings to six-years-old. Jake had had others help him work his mules previous years, but they always let some of the mules break away so Dad had told Jake he would bring over his boys and put the mules in the corral. I was only eight or nine but Dad said I could go along and ride drag—he even let me use one of the old army saddles that had leather cups over the stirrups so you couldn't get a foot caught.

It was only nine miles to Jake's and he didn't want to get started until eight o'clock in the morning, so we didn't have to hurry. We left home at seven and rode into Jake's yard at about ten minutes before eight. Army saddles are not really comfortable to ride in. There is no horn to hang onto and they have a gap down the middle (which I guess was meant so a rider could bounce in the saddle without bouncing on his privates). The stirrups hung off a narrow strap with a buckle in the middle of the strap just right to rub on the inner knee bone, and if that strap got a little slack and some skin happened to get between, why that would give a leg a hickey real fast. I had so many hickies on my legs by the time we go over to Jake's place that I would have rather rode bareback!

Jake was about ready to ride when we got there along with Leo and Oscar, who were there to help too. It seemed to me like a lot of riders just to get in maybe 35 mules and 25 horses, but Jake was determined to get them all in the corral that year. The older jack mules were getting mean, like a bunch of studs, always fighting and running something out of the bunch. Leo and Oscar were really good riders and Dad and my brothers Bob and Abe were too, so Jake, Abe, and me, took up the drag. I doubt if I was much help. I had to ride hard just to keep up with the herd of horses and mules. We took them in fast and they didn't have time to look for a wide-open space to break to. Leo, Dad, Oscar, and Bob were right on the ball and didn't let the bunch spread out any. In a short time, we managed to have every mule and horse in the corral, and it soon turned into an all-day job branding and cutting mules.

I had the easy job, just keeping the fire a burning and keeping the irons positioned in the fire so they got hot, but not the hand part, had to keep dirt over the iron so just the brand part got red hot. We got done about the time the sun was going down. Jake's wife Lizzie, who didn't have much good to say about anybody, stopped talking long enough to fix a big meal for us so we had to eat. Dad always would take time for a meal if one was offered, but I never figured out if it was just that Dad was half Scotch or if he was just afraid of what Lizzie might say to the neighbors if he said no to her cooking. By the time we were done eating and talking some extra too, it was good and dark. It didn't seem to bother Dad any that is was so dark you couldn't see much and we had to ride back home across some pretty rough terrain. We did ride some slower going home and it was well past bedtime when we got home.

Nick was good at helping about all the neighbors work cattle, and he was good at getting me to help him too. For several summers, I rode the eight miles up with him to Jim Petik's ranch, worked calves there, then rode back home that night. It usually took two days helping work cattle at Jim's and then we helped trail his cattle to pasture. His pasture was south of our place, around Black Horse Butte, only 12 miles or so but trailing calves that were still stiff from being worked made it a long 12 miles and used up all the daylight that there was in a day, plus a few extra hours of riding in the dark. Nick had promised me a calf for helping him each year, but that never happened, so Dad told me that after helping Nick for three summers I had better just stay home or work for someone else.

We were down in cow numbers and the horse market was so bad by 1951 he got rid of a lot of horses. Bob said those extra horses were just hay burners. That was the year he left and went into the Marines. Dad pastured cattle for other ranchers rather than try to get more of his own. Lowell Purdon had some cattle with Boyd Hall and they brought cattle over for summer pasture with Dad. Putting up hay with a team and mower was a slow process, but Bob did most of that so with him gone it was tough getting up enough hay for the cattle that we had. I drove a team on the mower some but guess I was a little young for Dad to trust me with that job. Most men would have been retired at Dad's age, but I suppose he wasn't ready to give up ranching.

Lowell came over to check on their cattle every

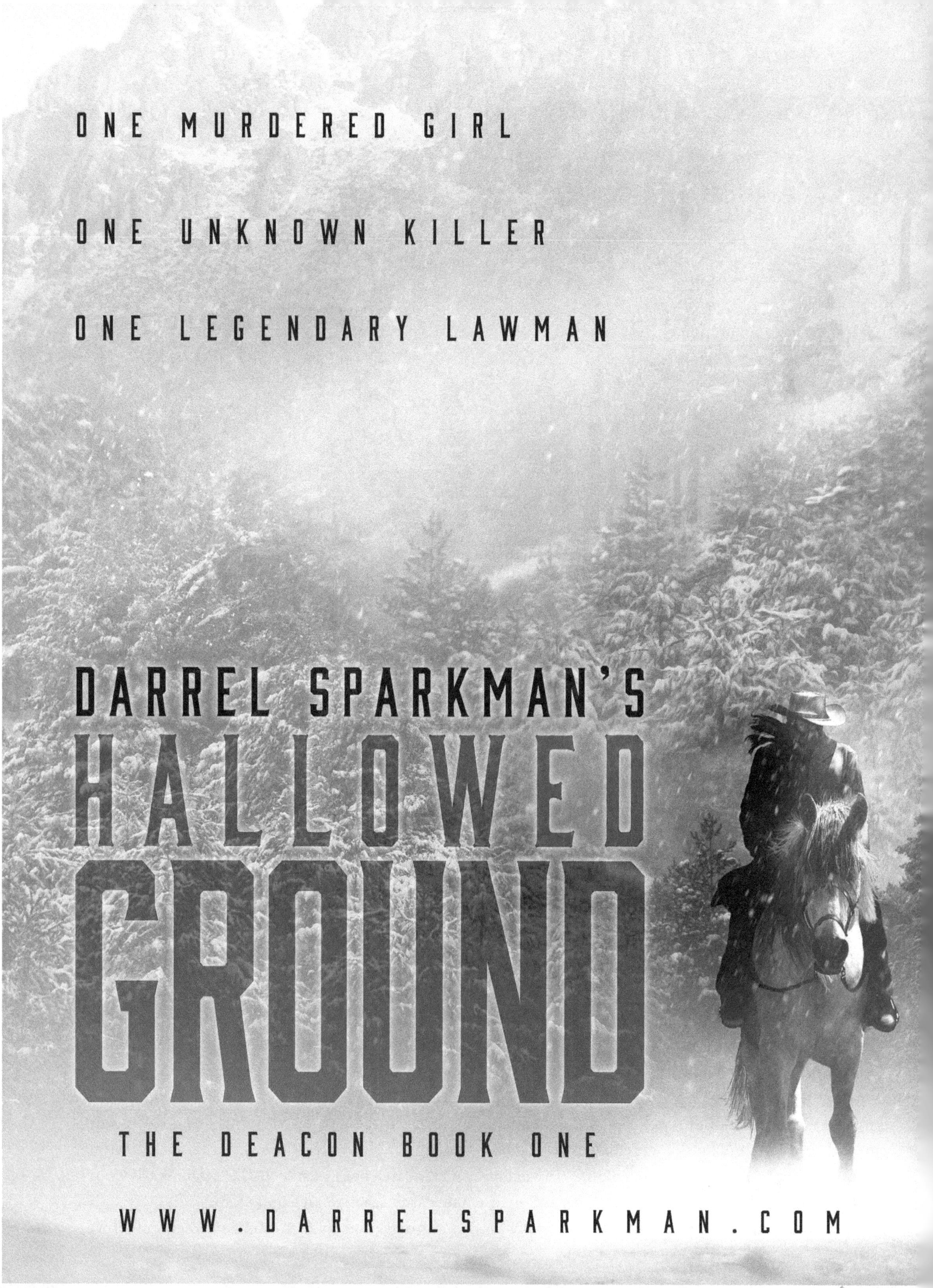

ONE MURDERED GIRL

ONE UNKNOWN KILLER

ONE LEGENDARY LAWMAN

# DARREL SPARKMAN'S
# HALLOWED
# GROUND

## THE DEACON BOOK ONE

WWW.DARRELSPARKMAN.COM

few days and really needed a chore boy, someone to get his cows in and help feed calves and hogs. He offered me a summer job helping him so I went over to his place and worked there for three summers until he sold the place. He did give me a calf each summer, and one time he gave me a colt and two pigs. He always paid me some money, and he was easy to work with—sometimes he was funny, too. He had good horses to ride and a good saddle too, but lots of times I would just run out and walk the milk cows in. Lowell's wife, Lois was the best cook, and she made me lots of western shirts. She called me "Dody," because Lowell had a sister, Iris, whose little girl, Carmen, couldn't say my name but called me Dody. Lois thought it was kinda cute, so she called me that too. I really liked all those shirts she sewed for me. They always fit better than ones from the catalog or general store.

Lowell and Lois sold their place when I was 15, so they left me with no job for the summer but not for long. Leo Anderson needed some help putting up hay and he hired me for the summer, but I quit in time to head back to school. Mom and the other kids rented a house in McIntosh for school but I liked the high school at Lemmon better. Lowell had taken a job as a cop in Lemmon and he and Lois offered me a free ride if I wanted to stay with them and go to high school. It didn't take me long to take them up on that offer—in Lemmon, I could play football and run track! Lowell even put in a good word for me at the Main Surplus Store—they needed a part-time helper and I got the job. Mostly I stoked the furnace and emptied ashes and stocked shelves. It was a pretty easy job and I got paid 75 cents an hour so I was like on easy street! The manager always liked to slip to the drug store for coffee and I had to manage the store while he was gone. Most stuff was marked but a few items weren't so he had told me if it wasn't marked that I should just pick a price out the air and if I did, to make sure it was high enough. Well, he was out to coffee and this lady came in and wanted to buy a wool blanket that didn't have the price marked. I stammered a little, then said that it was $3.79. She took it instantly and left. When the manager got back he said the blanket should have sold for $9.95. I told him he could take the difference

from my wages, but he didn't, however, we did get prices marked on more items after that.

Sometimes I rode around with Lowell in his police car, which brought out a few snide remarks from fellow classmates, but Lowell was about the best friend I ever knew, so I figured they were just envious. Lowell and Lois liked to go dancing, and square dancing was one of their favorites. Many times they would gather at someone's place and usually, Elmo Cain would come and do the calling for the square dance. If they were short one person to make a square, Lois would insist that I fill in, mostly with her partner. I was a bit bashful and wouldn't dance with the older women. At Ken and Esther Elson's place, we danced in one of their granaries but mostly they would just dance in someone's living room. Oscar Wiesinger and his brother Rudy would play and everyone would dance up a storm at those house parties. Oscar played guitar and accordion and Rudy was a fiddler. Guess I would have to credit Lois for teaching me how to dance or maybe making me dance. I was a slow learner, but after a few years, I managed to get the hang of it to some degree.

For the most part, high school was fun and easy enough. I wanted to go on to college when I graduated, but I didn't have much money, and my parents needed what they had just to get by. It cost over a $1,000 a year for tuition back in 1961. George Minges had offered to pay my tuition if I would go, but I was too afraid that something might happen. I might flunk out and I would still be short on money for books and clothes and trips back and forth—I was just too scared to try. After high school, I had a few cows with my brother Bob but didn't have enough to make a living with so I went to work out. I had 25 cows that I had been running at Leo Anderson's with his as part of my wages. That worked well for Leo and me too, but another uncle of mine—Uncle Sam—decided that I should come help him a couple of years, so I took my cows over to the home place and left them with Bob while I took care of some American missiles for two years in Germany.

A couple of months after I got out of the Army, I had just gone to work for Oscar Wiesinger, when a winter storm hit the area that lasted three days. It

was so bad you couldn't see ten feet outside. I lost about half of my cows to the storm. After that, I took 40 first-calf heifers on a share deal, but that was not a money maker, either. By the time I had paid pasture rent for those heifers, I ended up losing money. So I went down to Lead, South Dakota and worked in the gold mine there till I got tired of being a miner. The mine paid about four times as much as I could make working for ranchers. That lasted a year and a half and I got the bank paid back what I owed on the heifers and bought a new pickup.

The pay was good, but the work was hard and dirty and going 4,000 feet underground got old pretty fast, so I came back to Thunder Hawk and started working for others until I got enough cattle and money together to lease the home place. I worked for a couple of different farmers and bought ten heifers and increased my herd as I went along. In 1969 I leased the home place and bought a few more cows but still had to work for others to make ends meet. I managed to buy a quarter of land and increased my cow herd to some over a hundred in 1971. Each year I leased more land. I even leased a 133 acre irrigated pivot from Tom Lyman. Irrigating was a lot of work, but I had brothers that could help and we needed the extra hay for our increasing cattle herds. Agnes Howard was a widow who had land nearby with a 500 head range unit permit, and I leased her unit for three years. Bob and I leased a unit we called "Skull Butte," which was some 4,600 acres.

In less than 10 years, my ranch had grown from one of the smallest to one of the largest on the Standing Rock Reservation. I bought a place over in North Dakota about 30 miles west of Fort Yates in 1978. At that time, I owned a quarter of land and leased in the neighborhood of a township and a half, or roughly 50 sections—about 32,000 acres give or take a little.

Bob and I, along with Agnes, wintered over 800 cows plus bulls and replacement heifers. The early winter of 1977 was one of the hardest I can remember. The snow started early and lasted long with no breaks in the weather until the first part of March. I did lose 20 or so cattle from different things, mostly storm-related, and one saddle horse that got colic. One cow got pushed into the water tank and by the time I got her pulled out she was too cold to survive. Nine cows ate the tops off a choke cherry thicket and were poisoned and a bull died stuck in a snow drift. All and all, it was just a dang hard winter, but that comes with the territory. In the Dakotas, Mother Nature shows no mercy to man or beast. Dad raised a big family and kept us fed with 40 cows, but times had changed and are still changing. Dad put up hay with a team and horses. I had tractors, a swather, and a hydro-swing for putting up hay, not to mention pickups to drive. I had ten times as many cattle but the expenses took a big share of the income making the profit margin pretty darn small.

Hindsight is always 20-20, but it is a lot harder to see ahead with a clear vision. If I could have looked ahead down the trail, I would have seen that when you cowboy up, many days get long in the saddle and nights turn to morning fast. I am still trying to think of ways to repay all those good ole boys who encouraged me to be a cowboy. They seemed to know that I was tough enough for this life. I dang sure haven't passed any encouragement for the cowboy life onto my kids, but I do have two of the best, and I think they could have made it in the cowboy world.

If I could go back and do it over again, would I? Probably so!

*—George Gilland learned to be a rancher from his father, whose own father served under General Custer, at a time when cattle were still herded only by horseback and a close neighbor was eight miles away. He learned from friends and neighbors who taught the value of a hard day's ride and an honest days' work.*

*By the time he had kids of his own, his ranch covered more than 32,000 acres. George raised prize-winning cattle on the Standing Rock Sioux Reservation for more than thirty years and served as president of the Lakota Ranchers Association and treasurer of the American Indian Livestock Association. He is the co-author of two novels,* Along the Trail to Thunder Hawk *and* The Road Back to Thunder Hawk, *with his cousin and fellow member of Western Writers of America, Sharon Rasmussen.*

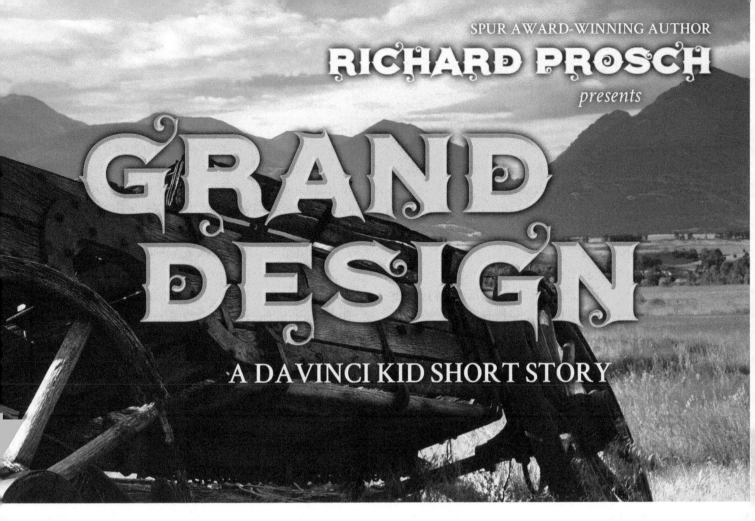

# RICHARD PROSCH

*presents*

# GRAND DESIGN

## A DAVINCI KID SHORT STORY

As one of the younger settlements on the Wyoming range, Randolph City's cemetery is small in acreage and big in sentiment. Spattered with wildflowers and smelling of cut grass, there's a wild beauty appropriate to the souls who rest there. The enormous gravestones are proportional—dad would say indirectly—to the character of those old timers. Founders (all men) whose pioneer spirits outshined the sordid details of their life.

It seemed impossible to bury 18 year-old Elly Benteen there.

Several years older, I was Elly's senior—but I could think of no place worse for my own eternal rest.

To bed down amongst the town fathers gave me the willies, as I'm sure it would Elly.

If she weren't dead, I mean.

Marching along with a solemn procession of mourners under a clear summer sky toward the graveyard's iron gates, I wondered what kind of marker Elly Benteen's father picked for her.

Big Sam, breeder of prize-winning stallions, was the second wealthiest man in the region, after Charles Murry. Sam Benteen could afford the best.

The summer wind pelted us with dust and next to me, Dad dabbed at his eyes.

"Be strong, Lacey," he said, and I gave his hand a squeeze. Marshal John Dale wasn't one to cry in public, but the loss of one so young and pretty to the fever had everyone in a tizzy.

Except, apparently, for my boyfriend Riley Boone who fidgeted under one of only two trees for miles around, next to the cemetery fence, next to one of the diggers, toeing the dirt pile and cocking his head to the left and right, watching with open curiosity as Elly's four old uncles lugged their dreadful cargo to the edge of a two foot riser.

They set the coffin down and I caught Riley's smiling eyes with a furrowed brow of my own.

*Show some respect, why don't you?*

He nodded a head of shaggy blonde hair, letting his wire-rimmed spectacles slide to the tip of his nose.

He silently mouthed something to me, surreptitiously pointing at the coffin.

I shrugged. "I don't understand," I whispered.

"Ours is not to understand the ways of the Lord," said dad, snuffing above his thick red mustache.

"I wasn't talking to you," I said.

At the gravesite, the line of three dozen dispersed, leaving the old folks and ladies to perch on a succession of wooden folding chairs set in place earlier in the day by members of the Congregational Church. The community leaders stood glumly at the side of the pit with the preacher. Big Sam commanded a position front and center, his round belly straining the buttons on a white silk shirt, his tall Stetson hat blocking the view of the ladies seated behind.

He stared at the hole in the ground with puffy red eyes.

"Where's Doc Hamilton?" I said, lifting my chin to scan the crowd. "Surely he'd be here?"

"With fever on the rampage, I s'pect he's got his hands full."

One dead girl wasn't much of a rampage, but I forgot the doc when I noticed a second face was missing.

Elly's four uncles, Sam's older brothers, Bob, Ed, Earl, and Ray, all in their middle to late 70s, bent to clasp the wrought iron casket hardware. With a heave, they brought the box to the cusp of the wood riser platform and slid it into place.

I could almost hear their backs creak. Earl let out a gasp, and each of them limped to the chairs reserved for them while the preacher took his place beside Elly's box.

While everybody got arranged, I scurried around to stand under the oak tree beside Riley. "Have you seen Doc Hamilton?" I said. "Or Charlie Murry?"

"How much would you say Elly weighed?" said Riley, not making any effort to whisper.

Or answer my questions.

Doc was President of the Chamber of Commerce. He should be here.

And as close as they were, it was impossible that Charlie wouldn't be present.

But I suspected Big Sam was just as glad. The Murry's cattle operation was twice the size of the Benteen operation, and the two families were bitter rivals.

"Romeo and Juliet," I mused with a smile, but literary allusions were lost on my male comrades.

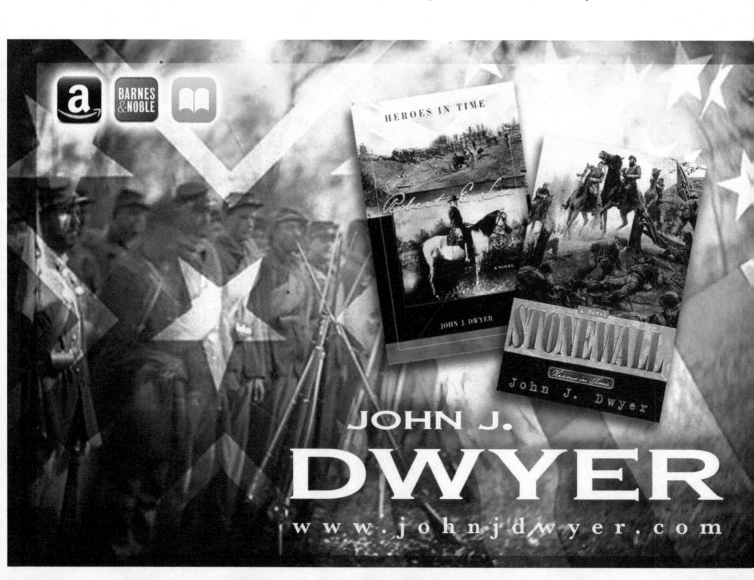

"Shush," whispered the clay-faced gravedigger at the fence. "We're gonna sing now."

"She wasn't a fat girl, was she?" said Riley. "Would you say Elly was fat?"

"Riley!"

"Certainly more than hundred pounds?" He scratched his head and watched a crow fly low over the seated crowd. "Maybe 130?"

"You best not let Big Sam hear you."

"I'd second that notion, friend," said the digger. "Take it from me, folks get mighty touchy about their dead. I mean, they could care less about somebody when they're alive and kicking, but after the drop off it's a whole 'nother story."

"We'll take that under advisement, thanks," I said.

"Would you say she was five feet tall? I think a bit more."

"More," I said. "Maybe five feet and four inches."

The assembled mourners started to sing "To Heaven I Lift Mine Eyes."

"Force times distance equals work," said Riley, gazing across the open prairie.

"Your boyfriend's quite a conversationalist," said the digger. "He always go on this way at funerals?"

Truth be told, I was just grateful Riley had taken the time to walk over and pay his respects.

I counted my blessings that he was dressed half-way decent.

That my dad had made Riley Boone a deputy law man a few months before when he'd helped to solve a series of baffling crimes was frequently forgotten. He was young, only a year older than me, and he spent most of his time cooped up in his clock shop on the edge of town –a building occupied twenty years before by Thomas Edison when that erstwhile personage traveled to Wyoming to watch a solar eclipse.

Edison left all manner of notes and forgotten inven-

VELDA
BROTHERTON

LAST RIDE
to
DEVIL'S
HOLE

a short story

tions that Riley tinkered with on a daily basis. To mangle an old saying, you could take the boy away from his science, but you couldn't take the scientist out of the boy.

"Mass times gravity equals weight," he said.

I nudged Riley in the ribs. "You didn't answer me about Doc Hamilton or Charlie Murry," I said.

"Under the willow," he said.

Following his gaze, I saw a lonely figure standing beside a horse under the open prairie's second tree.

"Why doesn't Doc join the crowd?" I wondered aloud. "You don't suppose he's quarantined himself?"

"That's just what I was thinking," said the digger with a serious nod. "Word is that it was him and only him that seen the girl after she passed. They didn't even let the undertaker have her for fear of contamination."

"Hence the closed casket," said Riley.

"Preacher's gonna talk," said Digger.

I'm not ashamed to say the Congregational minister wasn't familiar to me. He'd only recently moved to Randolph City with his family, and I haven't been much for churching since before my mom died.

With his puffed up shock of silver hair and syrupy way of talking, I didn't think I was missing much not making his acquaintance.

"The Good Book says there is a time for all things. For comings and for goings. A time to be born and a time to die. The idea that our beloved Elly Benteen departed this early veil too soon is but the judgement of sinful pride. The truth is the Lord needed another angel, and who are we to question His grand design."

"Who indeed," said the Digger with a sniff.

Riley held a pair of folding field glasses up to his spectacles. "I've got a question," he said.

saddlebag dispatches — 69

I took the glasses when he offered them. "Look at the saddle on Doc Hamilton's mount."

Ignoring the drone of the preacher, I stared through the magnifying lenses at the richly thick leather, the polished pommel, the ornately decorated skirt and billet straps. The roan horse was a wonder as well. Strong and sleek with muscles that rippled in the sunlight, he was the equal of any prize stallion Sam Benteen might own.

But it had a Murry Ranch brand.

"Doc Hamilton works strictly on barter," I said. "He doesn't have two cents to rub together." Handing the glasses back to Riley, I declared, "That must be somebody else's horse and saddle."

"Or perhaps the doctor has come into some money," he said.

The preacher had finished his piece and it was time to lower Elly into the ground. Again I watched her uncles teeter forward toward the coffin.

"Do you know that Bob and Earl helped me clean up some old iron behind the shop last week?" said Riley. "Neither of them can lift much of anything without giving out."

"So?"

"So if Elly weighs 130 pounds, plus something for the box—"

Before I knew it, Riley had taken three strides out of the oak tree's shade and rounded the mound of dirt.

I watched as he stepped in front of the four pall-bearers, stopping the service with an upturned hand. "If I might interrupt," he said. "For just a moment."

From his seat near the front, Dad spun around and gave me the stink-eye.

As if my impetuous friend's actions were my fault.

A gasp went up from the crowd as Riley bent down and knocked on the side of the box.

"Now. I won't stand for this," cried Big Sam.

"You won't have to," said Riley. "In fact," he said, straightening his back, "there's no need to continue with the service."

So transfixed was I with Riley's performance, I didn't notice the gravedigger move until he had a big knuckled hand firmly clamped around my boyfriend's arm.

"You stop this nonsense right now," he said. "You're just making it harder for these good folk."

Riley looked at Digger's hand like it was a specimen under a microscope.

With graceful ease, he slipped out of his jacket, leaving his frustrated attacker holding an empty sleeve.

Digger raised his shovel, might've dropped it on Riley's head too if not for my own interruption of the events.

The gun I carried under my petticoats was small

and only held two shots. But at close range it would shatter the man's forehead.

"And I expect that's something you don't particularly want," I said after explaining it to him. I smiled mischievously at Riley. "But it might be something Mr. Boone is gonna get if he doesn't explain himself."

Riley returned my smile and nodded back toward the willow tree outside the cemetery.

I looked just in time to see Doc Hamilton on his horse, riding away from the scene as fast as his new saddle could carry him.

With a nimble flourish, Riley shoved Digger aside and, gripping the coffin handle nearest him, turned the box over with a terrific crash. The lid sprang open, and the sorrowful contents exploded across the new mown grass.

Five pound bags of flour.

—

"**I suspect Charlie Murry** and Elly Benteen are off making a life for themselves by now," said Riley as he drew a dripping tea strainer by its chain from his steaming cup.

We sat together at Dad's kitchen table, the still gurgling kettle on a pad between us. Outside, the wind howled around the shutters and rattled the panes but the clear, starlit night was hardly forbidding.

In fact, it suggested a romantic dalliance under the moon. And The Marshal of Randolph City was having none of that.

"What I want to know is how you could be so doggone sure of yourself," said Dad, pulling up a chair.

"It's simply a matter of physics," said Riley. "The amount of force it would take to carry a heavy body and casket the distance those old men managed. The effort shown by those gentleman was almost Herculean when compared with what I've seen from them in the past."

"You don't think they noticed the load was lighter than it should've been?"

FINGERNAIL

MOON

A SHORT STORY

*by*

PAMELA

FOSTER

AUTHOR OF *BIGFOOT BLUES*

*Available for purchase exclusively on Amazon Kindle*

"You know the Benteen family hubris as well as anybody," said Riley. "I don't think their pride would let them admit it if they did."

"But still, you couldn't be sure. Can you imagine if you'd spilled the girl's body across the lawn in front of her grieving family? Not to mention exposing us all to the fever."

"There never was a fever, was there?" I said.

"I'm confident there wasn't," said Riley. "Remember the gravedigger said only Doc Hamilton had seen the girl. I suspect his diagnosis was part of the entire ruse. After pronouncing her dead, he spirited her away to the Murry ranch. Or perhaps Charlie was waiting for her outside Doc's office."

Riley sipped his tea.

"While the Benteen family thought Doc was preparing Elly for burial, she was miles away, in the arms of her lover. Heir to a rival family."

"Sam Benteen will demand a posse," said Dad. "He'll want Doc Hamilton tracked down. He'll want somebody to pay."

"Curious at Sam's reaction today," said Riley. "He seemed more angry at being tricked than joyful that his daughter wasn't deceased."

I put my hand on his arm. "Remember what the gravedigger said? Folks could care less about somebody when they're alive and kicking, but after the drop off it's a whole 'nother story."

"It's more than that and you know it," said Dad. "There was another quotation today at the gathering. What the preacher said—about questioning the grand design of things."

I thought about Elly Benteen as we sipped our tea and listened to the night outside, the crickets chirping, spring-peepers croaking, a coyote in the distance. All as much a part of the grand design as Elly Benteen and her lover.

And Sam would certainly be questioning that design tonight.

After all, Charlie—that is, *Charlene*—Murry was a girl.

# RICHARD PROSCH

Aﬀter growing up on a Nebraska farm, Richard Prosch has worked as a professional writer and artist while living in Wyoming, South Carolina, and Missouri. In the early 2000s, he won two South Carolina Press Awards and founded Lohman Hills Creative, LLC, with his wife, Gina.

Richard has written and published a multitude of short fiction, including three ongoing series of stories—Holt County, John Coburn, and Jo Harper. His western crime fiction captures the fleeting history and lonely frontier stories of his youth, where characters aren't always what they seem and the wind-burnt landscape is filled with swift, deadly danger.

In 2016, Richard won the Spur Award for short fiction presented by Western Writers of America for his short story, "The Scalper."

Richard and Gina live with their son, Wyatt, in Missouri.

Find out more about Richard and his work at **www.richardprosch.com.**

# *A HUNTING WE WILL GO....*

*You might say that the family that hunts together has a special camaraderie inspired by adrenaline-driven shared adventures. They never lack for exciting stories to tell while sitting around the campfire, and not least, they have no need to buy meat.*

*Elaine Marze*

Jeanette Clever, a Witter, Arkansas, grandmother says, "When I was growing up my family never bought meat at a grocery store." Due to a constant supply of quail, partridge, deer, elk, hog, buffalo, turkey, squirrel and so on, hunters like Clever and her family fill their freezers with wild game.

According to Jeanette's dad, Jesse Reynolds, he has hunted game all seventy-eight years of his life, which may be a slight exaggeration, but not by much. He also says he had his children in the woods hunting with him by the time they were three years of age. So, it is not too surprising that when he takes to the hills, most likely, at least one of his adult children accompany him. This is particularly true hunting wild boars in the Ozarks where they ride mules up and down the ravines after their prey accompanied by their faithful hunting dogs. Each family member has their own mules and dogs.

Why the preference for mules instead of horses? "Mules are tougher and more sure-footed," says Reynolds, "and when the going gets tough, mules will out-go horses every time. They don't flinch when you shoot off them. You don't have to train them to ignore gunfire. It's born in them."

Jesse has trailer-hauled his mules to Colorado and mule packed-in 30 miles or so to camp in the back-country hunting bear, elk, and deer. He's hunted mountain lions, bobcat, bear, deer, quail, pheasant, and elk in Idaho and Washington State with gun and bow. He's traveled to Alaska and Canada for moose and caribou. Jesse and his late brothers were known as the "Reynolds Mountain Mule Skinners".

Admittedly, more men than women hunt wild hogs, because, by anybody's standards, it can be dangerous, but Jesse claims, "Jeanette isn't afraid of anything. She'll ride her mule off a bluff or down the side of a mountain following a baying dog!"

JEANETTE, HER FATHER, JESSE REYNOLDS, AND ONE OF THEIR MULES ON A RECENT BOAR-HUNTING EXPEDITION.

"A few years ago I went on a seven-day cruise with my mother and sister, and I didn't have any fun. I hated it. Wild hog hunting is my idea of fun, and yes, hunting wild boars are the scariest thing I do, but it's also the most fun! The boars will try to get you so you want to be ready to climb a tree if you need to."

Stories abound of near misses and close calls while hunting wild boars and bears. Several times this family of hunters credits their dogs with jumping between them and attacking animals. Jesse has a nice bear skin rug he got after a bear chased him until he fell to the ground and when Jesse thought it was all over—his dog, Mac, "got the bear fighting him instead of chewing on me." While still on the ground, Reynolds rolled over and shot the bear, being careful not to hit Mac, whose back was broken in the fight. Thankfully, Mac lived to go on many more hunts.

Wild hogs will attack anything. They can also do a lot of property damage such as destroying gardens, so they are sometimes killed because of the nuisances they are instead of for their meat, but the Reynolds'

family eats what they kill. They do their own skinning and dressing of their kills, and Jesse is partial to the sausage he makes from wild game.

Hunting in the thickly-forested Ozark hills and rocky bluffs would intimidate most people, but it just adds to the adventure for the Reynolds family. After the dogs bay up a feral hog, a hunter usually gets off the mule to make his or her shot while the dogs hold the hog at bay. That is how the plan is supposed to work, but an experienced hog hunter will try to have an escape plan ready because sometimes the hogs go after the hunter. Once when a big boar came at Jesse he used the boar's momentum to throw the hog over his shoulder, but the enraged animal came back at him and went for his throat. Jesse held his arms up trying to protect his head, and "the boar grabbed one of my arms and tried to run off with it. That was one time I got chewed up pretty good," admitted Reynolds, "but my insulated coveralls helped protect me from a worse mauling."

Jesse and Jeanette have both had their dogs chewed up, but never fatally. An Airedale named

JEANETTE AND HER MULES.

Grunt had a habit of grabbing hogs by their ears until a big-tusked boar stabbed Grunt with its tusks puncturing an artery. "My brother took his shirt off to staunch the bleeding until we could pack him out to the veterinarian," Jesse said.

"The dogs are very loyal," says Jesse, a U.S. Army veteran. "They'll do anything to protect us." Think re-al-life enactment of the movie, *Old Yeller.*

During one wild hog hunt in the Buffalo River area, Jeanette's dog, Fishhook, now deceased, was with them even though, at the time, Fishhook was 13 years old but still eager to accompany the humans and four mountain curs along on this particular hunt. Once the dogs had the scent, the chase began that resulted in Jeanette killing a 350-pound boar. A slight problem arose though when the hog land-ed in an icy pond of freezing water. Jeanette tried to rope him to pull him out, but when that failed, she stripped down, waded in barefoot and pulled the hog out by the tail.

Another time, Jeanette broke her hand when she fell over a log while running from an attacking sow. One of the dogs had the sow penned and wouldn't let it loose so Jesse told Jeanette to catch the dog.

"When my daddy tells me to do something, I do it," said Jeanette. She got off her mule and had the dog by the tail pulling it off the sow when the sow decided to go after Jeanette. Then when Jeanette fell during the chase, it chewed on her leg until Jesse shot it. Between the humans yelling, the barking and pig

squealing, it got pretty loud in "them thar hills." It was a good thing that it was so cold—15 degrees—because the cold and Jeanette's many layers of clothes helped reduce her injuries. "And," she says, "I was lucky it was a sow and not a big boar with tusks!"

Because of the type of terrain in the hill country, many locals own and ride mules. Male and female mules are sterile. You get a mule from breeding a horse and a donkey. Crossing a male horse with a female donkey produces what is called a "jenny", a mule with shorter ears than a "jack", which is a male mule produced by breeding a female horse with a male donkey.

If you bring up the old adage about "stubborn as a mule" they are quick to tell you a mount needs to be stubborn to make it up and down the steep, rocky hills, bluffs, and ravines common to the Ozarks. The riders have to concentrate on staying in the saddles in such rough terrain so the more sure-footed their beast, the safer and more relaxing the ride. This area of Arkansas is referred to by lots of people as, "God's Country", and according to the Reynolds Mountain Mule Skinners, a man can't ask much more of life than to live here where the hunting is plentiful, with a good mule to ride and dogs eager to track!

—*Elaine Marze is a newspaper and magazine journalist who has also authored three non-fiction books,* Hello Darling *and* Widowhood: I Didn't Ask for This, *inspirational humor written about the traditionally non-humorous subjects of cancer and widowhood.*

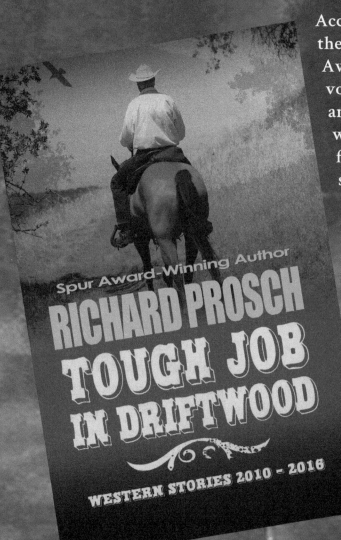

# HANNAH'S DAUGHTERS

### a short story by STEPHEN CARR

Standing on an overlook above a stretch of a prairie, wind whipped Leila's dress, causing the material to make noises like fingers being snapped. She tightened the knot under her chin of the cord attached to her hat and adjusted her gun belt. Squinting from the glare of the sun, she watched as a small herd of bison made their way through tall brown prairie grass. As bits of dirt battered her face, she turned her head toward the sun-bleached rock formations that rose from the prairie in the far distance like mountains that had been stepped on and broken into pieces by the foot of God.

"Are we close?" Sarah asked from the seat of the wagon and holding the reins to the two horses. There was a rigidity to the way she sat, as if her spine had been replaced with a column of stone. In her face there was none of the freshness of a girl of nineteen. She had the haggard and wary look of an aging coyote.

"Very close," Leila said. She took another look toward the bison. They had disappeared, camouflaged by the colors of the dry earth and sunburnt grass. Familiar with how the landscape could play tricks on an untrained pair of eyes, she kept her focus on

where they had last been seen. Within minutes their movement was detected even before she made out their hulking brown forms, as if they had been swallowed by the prairie and were being spit up from it. She got back in the seat of the wagon and took the reins from Sarah's hands. She lightly slapped the reins on the sides of their necks.

"Giddyup there," she called out.

As the horses began to trot through the grass, their hooves kicking up small clouds of dirt, Sarah removed her bandana releasing her long, dark brown, oily hair that hung down the sides of her face like dirty thread. "I remember none of this," she said.

"You were very young," Leila said raspily. She spit soil from her mouth over the side of the wagon. A small brown streak of it dribbled down her chin. "I remember almost every blade of grass."

Sarah leaned back and looked up at the scattered balls of snow-white clouds in the baby blue sky. "It hasn't rained since we left Kansas City. What I wouldn't give for a bath."

"That's how it is on the plains," Leila said. "You could have stayed home."

"I could have," Sarah said. She put the bandana back on her head and tied the two ends together under her chin. "Sixteen years is a long time to be away from a place. You think it's changed much?"

"Places change but the people in them rarely do," Leila said.

As the horses stepped out of the grass and onto a dirt road, Leila said, "We'll be there shortly. Get in the wagon and change into something more respectable looking. I'll stop the wagon just before entering town and you can get out the back."

"Okay," Sarah said. Before climbing under the white canvas cover she said, "It's been nice knowing you."

—

**Bliss Atkins put a** glowing red horseshoe on the anvil with the tongs and lifted a hammer and brought it down on the shoe. The smashing of metal on metal rang out discordantly, reverberating in the stable.

White sparks sprung up from where the hammer struck the shoe. He hit the shoe again, then lifted it with the tongs and examined both sides, then tossed the shoe into a bucket of water. Wisps of steam rose out of the water accompanied by hissing like that of an angry snake. He leaned against a beam that held up the roof and tried to ignore the rivulet of hot sweat that was running down his back.

Leila pulled her wagon to a stop at the open front door of the stable. She watched him for a minute as he wiped sweat from his forehead and eyes with a bandana before saying anything. His appearance hadn't changed since the last time she saw him. He was the definition of brute strength and ugliness. "Where can I tie up my wagon and stable my horses?" she said.

Bliss removed the bandana from his eyes and ran his knuckles down the long, thin red scar on his cheek that ran from below his right eye to his chin. "Where's your man?" he said. He eyed her in the way a coyote eyes a rabbit.

# BIG FOOT
## Mamas

*"Few writers can capture the beauty and emotion of a single moment like John Steinbeck could... and yet Pamela Foster does it with every turning page."*

### a novel

## pamela foster
### author of *Bigfoot Blues*

"I have to have a man to take care of my wagon and horses?" she said.

He flashed a smile that quickly vanished. "I just don't get many women who come here on their own pulling a wagon," he said. He placed the tongs on the anvil and stepped out of the stable and stood beside the wagon looking up at her. He laid his massive hand on the wagon floorboard perilously close to her boot. "You look kinda familiar. You been here before?"

"No," Leila said. "I'm just passing through and heading west." In her head she was hearing the breaking of his fingers as she crushed them beneath her heel.

"All alone? With Indians still on the loose?" he said. Despite his looks, he wasn't a stupid man. He pulled his hand from the floorboard and momentarily let it hang in the air like a wounded hawk before dropping it to his side.

She put her hand on the handle of her gun. "I can take care of myself." She hadn't seen an Indian since leaving Kansas City and half-wondered if they had mostly been driven from the open plains just like the buffalo.

"That gun ain't going to save you if you're being chased by a dozen of them savages."

"That's my concern, isn't it?"

He scratched his scar again. "I guess it is. You can pull your wagon into the paddock behind my stable and I have room for your horses." He stepped back from the wagon while staring at her face. He knew he had been lied to, that they had met before, but he couldn't place when or where. He saw so few new faces that the ones he had seen were seared into his brain as if branded there.

"Thanks," she said.

"You sure we haven't met before?"

"Certain of it," she said.

—

**Standing in the doorway** of the drygoods store, Lizzy fanned her face with the lid from a tin of crackers. An eddy of dirt whirled across the street, falling apart just as it hit the wood walkway a few feet in front of her. She brushed from her apron the flour that had spilled onto it causing a white cloud that was blown back into her face. She wiped her face with her hand

and turned facing the dimly lit interior of the store. Dan Blevins, the store owner, was behind the counter, his head bowed over a ledger as he mumbled numbers aloud. His bent shoulders reminded her of those of a turkey vulture. He looked up from the ledger and looked at her over the tops of wire rim glasses that rested on the end of his nose.

"You done with your work?"

His face fascinated her. It had the look of a man who was born with wrinkles—he came out of his mother's womb old. Although only about twice her age, whatever youth there may have once been in him had dried up long ago. With the light from the oil lamp cast on the ledger and one half of his face, the wrinkles hidden in the shadows were like dry gulleys. "Yes, all done except for sweeping the floor."

"Get to it. I don't pay you to stand around gawking."

She took one more look out the door. Walking down the middle of the street carrying a threadbare purple carpetbag was her twin sister, Sarah.

She grabbed the broom beside the door and quickly swept the dirt and flour in the doorway out onto the walkway where the hot wind caught it and spread it across the walkway's boards like drifting sand. At the railing, Lizzy looked over her shoulder to make sure Dan wasn't watching her, and tapped the broom handle against the wood rail three times.

Sarah casually turned her head and without pausing in her steps, nodded imperceptibly.

Lizzy lazily brushed the straw of the broom over the boards as peripherally she watched Sarah leave the street and step up onto the walkway and enter the hotel.

"This store won't sweep itself," Dan called out from inside.

Lizzy carried the broom inside.

—

**At the counter of** the High Winds Hotel, Leila slapped the palm of her hand down on the small upside down bowl shaped bell. The bell chimed like an empty tin can being struck with a wooden shoe horn, but it was surprisingly loud and echoed in the lobby. Painted a pale rose color and simply furnished with one chair and a large mirror on one wall, other than the counter where guests checked in, the lobby served no purpose and was almost never used. Because of its paint, it was the prettiest place in High Winds. Within a minute Hurse Margrove opened the door behind the counter and stepped out, pulling the door closed behind him. He hastily shoved his arms into the sleeves of his ill fitting coat and smiled wanly at Leila. Remnants of the charred beef he had been eating in the back room coated his teeth.

"Can I help you Madam?"

"I'll be needing a room."

He rubbed his coat sleeve across his lips and unsuccessfully tried to hold back a belch. It came out sounding more like a squeak.

"Excuse me," he said sheepishly. He locked eyes with hers as if trying to recall something. "Is this your first time in High Winds?"

"Yes," Leila said. "I'm heading west."

"The stagecoach isn't due until tomorrow," he said. "How did you get here?"

"By covered wagon."

"Dangerous way to travel," he said. "Your husband handy with a rifle?"

"I'm not married," she said. "I'm traveling alone."

Hurse tilted his bald head and stared at her appraisingly. He had seen many strangers check into the hotel over the years and few of them who came through High Winds were model citizens wherever they had left. "If the law is after you it's better to let them catch you then risk being alone going across the prairie."

"They're not. May I have a room?"

He flipped a page in the ledger on the counter, dipped a pen in the inkwell and handed it to her. As she signed her name he leaned over the counter and peered down at her small brown leather suitcase sitting by her feet. "You travel light."

"I'm a woman of simple tastes."

Hurse turned and took a key out of the box numbered "5" and handed it to her. He was about to

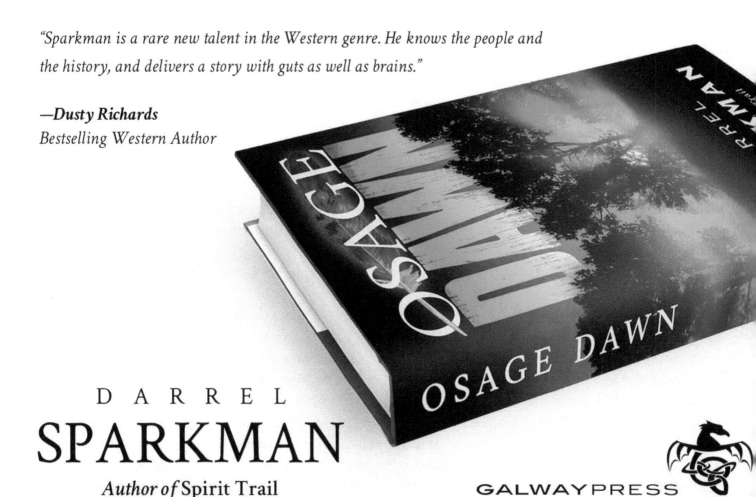

offer to carry her bag up the stairs for her when the front door opened and the bell above it tinkled. A young woman carrying a purple carpet bag entered. He turned to see Leila going up the stairs carrying her suitcase. Before the young woman got to the counter he looked at the ledger.

*Leila Prescott* was written in bold lettering on the top line of the otherwise blank page.

At the top of the stairs, Leila stopped and watched as Sarah stepped up to the counter.

"I'll be needing a room," Sarah said.

—

**While leaning on the** sill of the open window of his office, Sheriff McDill had watched Leila drive her wagon into town and down the street. Thinking her husband was probably inside the wagon, he stopped watching as soon as the wagon had passed by. Then a half hour later he watched Sarah stroll into town carrying the purple carpetbag. A young woman walking into town all alone made no sense at all. High Winds was practically in the middle of nowhere. There wasn't a place within walking distance, to walk from or to. She carried the carpetbag as if she had been born with it attached to her hand. And he was certain that he had seen the bag before.

Leaving the window, he sat in the squeaking chair at his desk and thumbed through the "Wanted" posters that had been neglected for weeks. In the stack there were only men on the run from the law. He leaned back and put his boots up on the desk and with his hands behind his head stared up at the thin cracks in the gray ceiling feeling his gut being twisted. In a town with sixty people there wasn't much to worry about until strangers came to town who didn't come in by stagecoach.

When dust began to blow through the open window he raised the bandana that had been tied around his neck up to his mouth and got up and opened the office door.

Westward, a curved wall of dust stretched across the horizon from the ground to the sky and it was barreling across the plains and headed straight for High Winds. The thunder from the storm rumbled like a thousand Indian drums.

—

**Lizzy pulled the shutters** across the store's plate glass window then went inside and pulled the door closed. She brushed the dirt and bits of prairie grass from her dress then took her bandana from her head and shook it. The lighter tin cans on the shelves trembled with each roll of thunder. She dipped the metal ladle into the barrel of fresh water and as she drank from the ladle she stared at Dan who was at the counter with the cash register drawer open and counting money. She dropped the ladle into the barrel.

"You knew my mother," she said.

He continued counting coins. They clanked as they were dropped from his hand into a small burlap bag.

Lizzy came nearer to the counter. "You knew my mother," she said again.

He stopped counting "Your mother?" he said. "You're not from here so how could I have known your mother?"

Wind screeched through the spaces between the boards at the front of the store.

"My mother was Hannah Carson."

"Hannah Carson? Never heard of her." He tied a piece of red yarn around the top of the bag.

"Sixteen years ago my family was going to homestead on a piece of land not far from town," she said. "The western boundary was the overlook."

"What's it to me?" He removed the glasses and held them in his hand, running his fingertips across the glass.

"You and two other men raped and murdered her," Lizzy said.

"You're crazy," he said as he slammed the register drawer closed.

Lizzy pulled a .455 Webley from the pocket in her dress and aimed it at him. "A fourth man told my father what happened and who was involved."

As he started to grab the gun he kept on the shelf under the counter, Lizzy shot him in the right shoulder. He fell back against shelves of tobacco and bottles of whiskey behind the counter.

"Let me explain."

"There's nothing to explain."

The building shook as the wall of dust and dirt battered it. She shot him again, between the eyes.

He slid to the floor gripping onto his broken glasses.

—

**The shutters over the** hotel's lobby windows shook as the wind and dust smashed into them.

Standing behind the counter, Hurse slurped large spoonfuls of beef soup into his mouth. A thin layer of grease on the top of the soup had the look of pond scum. After each spoonful he loudly smacked his lips with satisfaction. When Sarah came down the steps and stood in front of the counter he didn't bother to stop eating.

"My sister said you were still in town."

He swallowed a fatty chunk of beef. "Your sister?"

"She arrived here a couple of weeks ago by stage," Sarah said. "I think she stayed here a couple of nights."

"Who's your sister?" he said as he wiped his mouth with his sleeve.

"We're identical twins," she said. "I'm surprised you didn't mention her when I checked in."

"I don't really pay attention to what folks look like," he said. "Although the woman who checked in just before you arrived looked somewhat familiar."

"She's a relative of ours," Sarah said. She raised her hand that she had been hiding in the folds of her skirt. In it was a Webley Bull Dog Pocket Revolver. She aimed it at his head.

He slowly put the soup spoon into the bowl of soup. "Is this a holdup?" he stammered as his jowls wobbled.

"No, it's not. This is revenge for what you and two other men did to my mother," she said.

"Your mother?" Hurse said. "Who was your mother?"

"Hannah Carson." She pulled the trigger. As the bullet struck him in the forehead he crashed back against the boxes with the room keys.

Leila came down the stairs carrying her suitcase and Sarah's purple carpetbag.

"Feel better?" she asked Sarah.

"A little," Sarah said.

Leila handed the purple bag to Sarah, then opened the door. The last of the storm blew dirt through the opened door.

—

**As he slid open** the door to the stable, Bliss saw the two women crossing the street heading his direction. Watching the way the older woman walked made him realize who she was. He thought about quickly closing the door and locking it, but they both raised their hands and aimed their guns at him. The closed door wouldn't stop the bullets if they decided to shoot. He raised his hands over his head.

"Why'd you do it?" Leila said.

"It wasn't me, it was them. They wanted to make sure that land along the overlook wasn't homesteaded," he said. "They planned on building on it themselves as High Winds got bigger. They figured with Hannah out of the way her husband would take the children and leave."

"It worked," Leila said.

"You have to believe me, I had nothing to do with it," he said as he backed up and they stepped into the stable.

"You could have stopped it," Leila said, pointing her Colt Walker Revolver at his head.

"I tried," he said. "That's how I got this scar on my face. "Dan Blevins said he'd cut my throat if I interfered." He stared at Leila. "You remember how mean Dan was back then."

"Hold it right there." It was Sheriff McDill. He was standing a few yards behind Leila and Sarah and had his rifle aimed at them. "Either of you make a move and I won't hesitate to shoot you in the back. Now turn around."

The two women slowly turned, facing the sheriff.

"What's this all about?" Sheriff McDill asked.

"Hannah," Bliss said. "They've come to settle the score."

"That so?" the sheriff said. "Why are you two?"

"Us three." Lizzy stepped behind the sheriff and put the barrel of her pistol in the middle of his back. "Drop your rifle."

Sheriff McDill turned his head slightly to look at Lizzy. "Hannah had two sons," he said. He raised his rifle.

Just as Leila shot him in the lower back with her revolver, he instinctively pulled the trigger on the rifle. The bullet caught Bliss in the chest killing him instantly.

"Quickly, get the sheriff out of the street," Leila said.

Sarah and Lizzy each took one of his legs and dragged him into the stable and closed the door. He lay on his back, a trickle of blood running out of the side of his mouth.

"Get the hair scissors and our clothes out of the bags," Leila pointed her pistol at his head. "Make sure to put your mother's carpetbag back in the wagon."

"Luke Carson?" Sheriff McDill mumbled looking up at Leila.

Leila nodded. "It took the boys and I six months to grow our hair and learn how to act and sound like females. No one between here and Kansas City saw or met anyone who fit our real descriptions."

"What now?" the sheriff said.

"We continue on west, and from the look of things High Winds will probably turn to prairie dirt soon enough," Luke said. "What you did to my wife was all for nothing."

"If it's any consolation, Hannah fought like a wild cat the entire time," Sheriff McDill said.

Luke shot him in the head.

# STEPHEN CARR

Steven Carr, who lives in Richmond, Virginia, began his writing career as a military journalist. Interested in theater, his first writing successes were his plays, many of which were staged in Albuquerque and Cincinnati. He didn't turn to writing short stories until June, 2016. He very quickly found his stories appearing in publications such as *Fictive Dream, Rhetoric Askew* and *Storyland Literary Review*. He has had over 170 short stories published internationally in print and online magazines, literary journals and anthologies to date. *Sand*, a collection of his short stories, was published recently by Clarendon House Books and is available for purchase on Amazon and elsewhere.

For more information on Steven go to his website at **www.stevecarr960.com**, or find him on Twitter @carrsteven960.

"Hannah's Daughters" is Steven's first story to appear in the pages of *Saddlebag Dispatches*.

# bender

SCRIPT BY MICHAEL FRIZELL

ART BY D. A. FRIZELL

Prof. Miss KATE BENDER!
...n heal all sorts of Diseases; can cure ...
... Fits, Deafness and all such diseases...
...and Dumbness. ...
...nce, 14 miles East of Ind...
...n Independence...
...iles Sou...

BOOK FIVE: SPIRIT GUIDE

1873: OUTSIDE FORT SCOTT, KANSAS

WELL, DOCTOR YORK? THIS THE WAGON YOU SOLD TO THAT LOCHNER FELLA?

IT IS. SOLD IT TO HIM ABOUT A MONTH AGO FOR A FAIR SUM.

I FEARED THE WORST WHEN I HEARD THE WAGON HAD BEEN FOUND WITHOUT ITS NEW OWNER.

THE HOMESTEADER OF THIS PARCEL'A LAND FOUND THE HORSE TIED TO THE TREE. NO TELLIN' HOW LONG IT'S BEEN HERE, BUT THE HORSE'S STARVIN' AND LOOKS TO NOT BEEN WATERED FOR A WEEK.

TAKE CARE'A IT. IT'S SUFFERED ENOUGH.

...AND NO SIGN OF...

KA-BLAM!

...OF...GEORGE OR HIS DAUGHTER?

WELL, WE DID FIND SOME CLOTHING IN THE WAGON THAT BELONGED TO A MAN AND A GIRL: A SUIT...PINK AND WHITE DRESS.

TRAIL'S LONG COLD, I'M AFRAID. YOU SAID HE WAS HEADIN' TO...?

9

VON'T YOU SIT, COLONEL?

JOHN! GET UP UNDT LET ZE COLONEL SEET.

NO, NO THAT WON'T BE NECESSARY, MISS BENDER, BUT THANK YOU. I JUST HAD A FEW QUESTIONS.

I WANTED TO ASK YOU ABOUT A MISTER WILLIAM JONES. HEARD'A HIM?

NEIN.

WELL, IT'S A NASTY SORT'A BUSINESS, MISS BENDER. I HESITATE TO DESCRIBE THE CONDITION WE FOUND HIM IN, BUT HE WAS FOUND ON DRUM CREEK IN 1871...

...JUST ABOUT THE TIME YA'LL ARRIVED.

HE'D BEEN ROBBED. SOMEONE TOOK HIS BELT, HIS SHOES, HIS WALLET...ANYTHING OF VALUE...

HIS HEAD WAS CAVED IN FROM THE BACK. LIKELY NEVER SAW HIS ATTACKER.

<URR-HEH> D-DRUM? ZE CREEK?

YES.

DANGEROUS CROSSING ZERE, YES?

<HEH-HAH> MOST DANGEROUS. I VAS ACCOSTED ZERE LAST YEAR.

OH? I KNOW IT'S EARLY, SIR, BUT, YOU THINK YOU CAN SHOW ME WHERE?

<URRM-HEH> JA. JA. EET VAS --

- HERE. <URR-HUH> HERE. ZE MEN...ZERE VERE ZWEI... <URR> TWO. ZEY HIT ME. TOOK...MY MONEY FOR MARKET.

ZEY...<URR-HA-HAH> ZEY VERE NOT KNOWN TO ME. I NOT <HURGH-HA> GET LOOKIT FACES, NEIN. AND I <URR-HEH> I...<HEH> I...<URGH-HUH>

ALL RIGHT, MISTER BENDER. ALL RIGHT

SORRY TO MAKE YOU HAVE TO RELIVE THAT, BUT WE HAD TO KNOW FOR SURE. YOU CAN GO BACK TO YOUR PA. I'VE HEARD WHAT I NEEDED.

GUY'S TOUCHED.

QUITE. STILL, HIS STORY CHECKS OUT.

YOU...BELIEVE HIM, COLONEL?

CAN'T SEEM TO FIND A REASON NOT TO. SURE, THEIR LANGUAGE COULD BE CAUSIN' SOME CONFUSION, BUT...WELL...AFTER TALKIN' TO THE FOLKS IN THESE PARTS, THE KEEPER AT THE CHERRYVALE HOTEL, WHERE KATE WORKED, THAT ERN FELLA AT THE GENERAL STORE, AND PASTOR DICK, I JUST CAN'T SEEM TO FIGURE THEM AS GUILTY PARTIES HERE.

"THEY JUST SEEM LIKE SIMPLE, CREDULOUS FOLK."

"THERE IS NO LONGER ANY DOUBT IN THE MINDS OF THE PEOPLE OF THIS TOWNSHIP THAT A DREADFUL CRIME OF SOME NATURE HAS BEEN PERPETRATED.

...WHAT THE...? WHOAH, BOY. EASY.

"HENRY HOSTETTER OF SW COAL COMPANY SAYS HE SAW A MAN AT THE WAGON THREE TIMES BEFORE THE HORSES WERE BROUGHT UP TO TOWN IN HIS SHIRT SLEEVES

MAY 1, 1873.

...GOD...

"AND SEVERAL OTHERS SAW A MAN THERE WITH HIS COAT ON.

"A FEW DAYS LATER, SEVERAL MEN ORGANIZED BY COLONEL YORK FOUND THE WAGON HIDDEN IN WHEELER'S STABLE.

"ON THE BOTTOM OF THE WAGON WE SAW A PIECE OF FLOORING BOARD NAILED OVER A HOLE ON WHICH WAS DAUBED IN CRUDE LETTERS, GROCRY.

"PULLING THIS OFF, WE FOUND ON THE OTHER SIDE THE SAME STYLE --

"GROCERY.

BENDER? YOU ABOUT? IT'S BILL...BILLY TOLE... YOUR NEIGHBOR!

KATIE?

"THE WAGON WAS CONSIDERABLY WORN, THE HIND WHEELS ARE BOTH DISHED THE WRONG WAY BY BEING TOO HEAVILY LOADED AND TWO OF THE SPOKES OF THE RIGHT HIND WHEEL ARE BROKEN.

"IT HAS NOW BEEN ELEVEN DAYS SINCE THIS WAS FOUND, AND NO LIGHT HAS BEEN THROWN ON THE MYSTERY YET.

"LAST MONDAY WEEK, THE WAGON WAS BROUGHT U[P] FROM THE RAVINE NEAR TOWN AND IN IT WAS FOUN[D] A DOUBLE BARRELED SHOTGUN. ONE BARREL WAS LOADED AND THE OTHER EMPTY.

...MISTER BENDER?

"THE ONE THAT WAS LOADED HAD A CHARGE OF BUCKSHOT ON TOP OF AN ORDINARY LOAD OF COMMON SHOT.

"THE SIDE OF THE WAGON BOX WAS FULL OF SHOT.

GOVERNOR'S PROCLAMATION

$2,000 REWARD

State of Kansas, Executive Department.

WHEREAS, several atrocious murders have been recently committed in Labette County, Kansas, under circumstances which fasten, beyond doubt, the commissions of these crimes upon a family known as the "Bender family," consisting of

JOHN BENDER, about 60 years of age, five feet eight or nine inches in height, German, speaks but little English, dark complexion, no whiskers, and sparely built;

MRS. BENDER, about 50 years of age, rather heavy set, blue brown hair, German, speaks broken English;

JOHN BENDER, Jr., alias John Gebardt, five feet ... inches in height, slightly built ... brown hair, light ... moustache ... age, speaks English ...

KATE BENDER ... ... speaks ... well ...

"WE HOPE PAPERS THROUGHOUT THE COUNTRY WILL CALL ATTENTION TO THIS."

END BOOK FIVE.

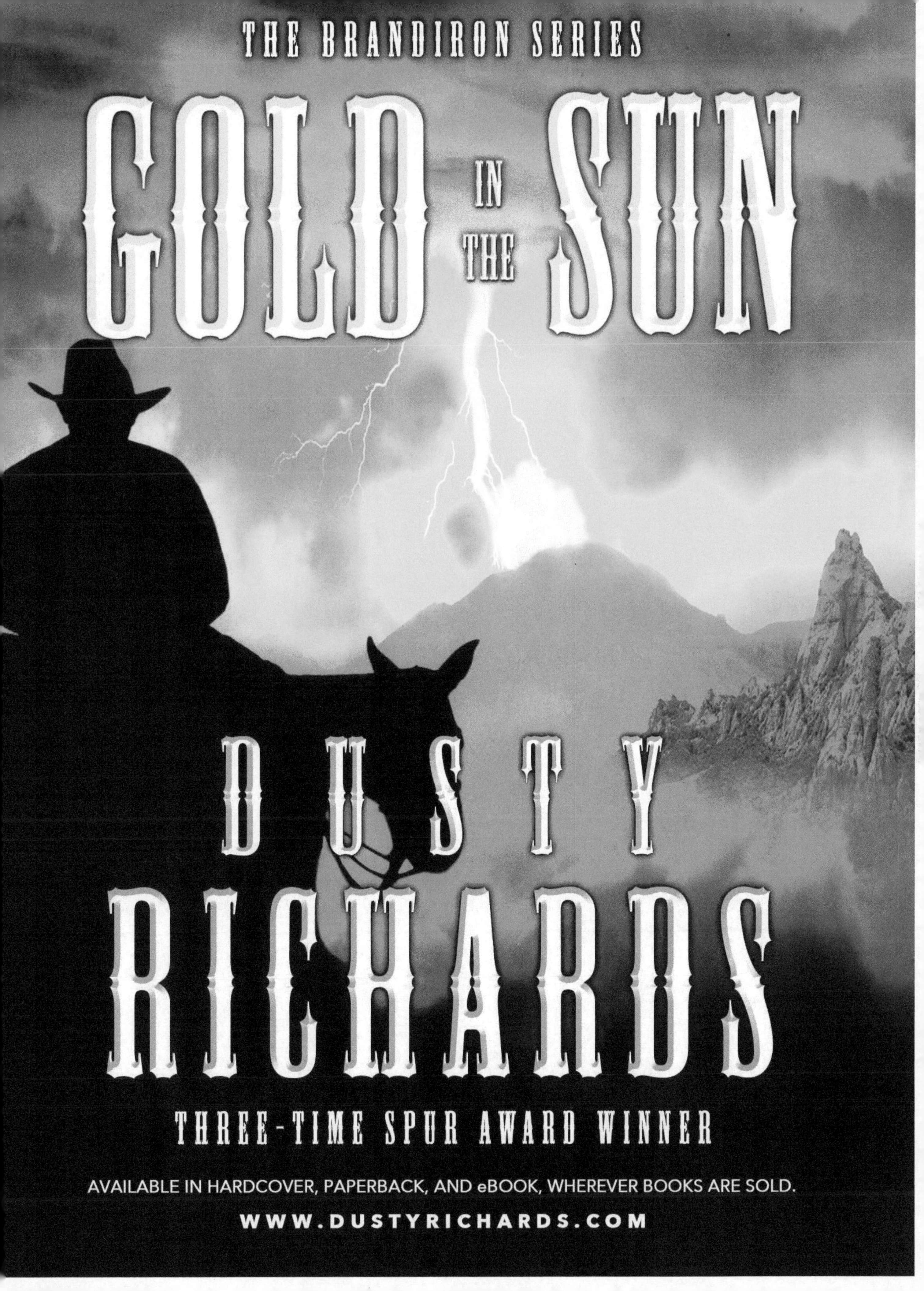
THE BRANDIRON SERIES
GOLD IN THE SUN
DUSTY
RICHARDS
THREE-TIME SPUR AWARD WINNER
AVAILABLE IN HARDCOVER, PAPERBACK, AND eBOOK, WHEREVER BOOKS ARE SOLD.
WWW.DUSTYRICHARDS.COM

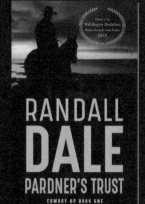
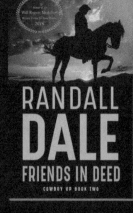
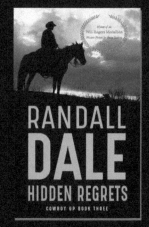
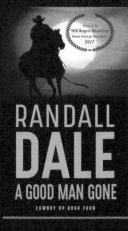

# LUCY'S GOLD

*a short story by*

# JOHN M. FLOYD

hat did you do?" Lucy asked.

The young man in the seat across from her made no reply. He just sat there, staring out the window of the stagecoach.

A while ago, when Lucy Roberts climbed into the stage in Heritage, she stumbled a bit on the step, and he had leaned forward to take her hand. Their eyes met then, but he didn't speak—in fact he'd hardly looked at her since.

But she had looked at him. The truth was, she had scarcely taken her eyes off him. He was intriguing, Lucy thought—sandy hair, square chin, blue eyes. And about her age, nineteen or so. She found herself wondering if this feeling, this—fascination, almost — might be more than just a passing interest. If it was, there were two things here that could prove to be a little inconvenient. One was that she was already engaged to be married; the other was that he was wearing a pair of handcuffs.

Whatever the case, Lucy thought, he should have the courtesy to answer her question. But just as she opened her mouth to ask him again, he turned from the window and looked at her. She snapped her mouth shut.

"Did I miss something?" His voice was deep, his eyes tired.

Lucy cleared her throat. "I asked you a question."

"Would you care to repeat it?"

"I asked you," she said, with a glance at his handcuffs, "what it was that you did."

Another long pause. Then: "They say I robbed a railroad office." The tiredness in his face seemed to deepen, and he turned again to the window.

"What do you mean 'they say'? Did you or didn't you?"

Again, no response. They rode on in silence.

Finally the third passenger—the man sitting beside the prisoner—spoke up.

"His name's Charlie McCall," the man said. "He was outside, holding his two friends' horses, when the two run out of the office with the stolen money. They was both shot dead, and McCall here was charged as their accomplice." He paused, then added, "He said he hadn't known anything about a robbery."

Lucy studied the older man a moment. He was burly, with a red face and mustache. A sheriff's star was pinned to his vest.

"Are you telling me he's innocent?" she asked.

The sheriff shrugged. "Don't matter what I tell you. We're on our way to Dodge, to let the judge decide. It's what he'll tell us that matters."

Lucy nodded in Charlie McCall's direction. "I want to know what he would tell me."

The big sheriff chuckled. "He won't tell you nothing, less he's looking at you when you ask him."

"What?"

"He's deaf," the sheriff said.

She blinked. She turned to the young man again, watching him watch the plains roll past outside the stage's long window. She remembered now: his eyes had been fixed on her lips as she spoke to him.

"His pa was killed in a mine blast, years ago," the sheriff said. "Young Charlie was with him at the time. The boy survived, but could never hear again. Came to live with his aunt outside Heritage." The sheriff squinted. "You're from Heritage yourself, ain't you? A clerk at the bank?"

She nodded, looking at the sheriff but still thinking about Charlie McCall. "Until it closed," she said. "Mr. Larrabee's opening a new bank in Dodge, and said I could work for him again. I'm on my way there now, with the last of his move."

"His move?"

She hesitated. "I'm bringing the rest of his gold. It's in a strongbox, up top." Lucy was aware that the young man had turned from the window and was watching her as she spoke. She found it hard not to look at him.

"You mean you're making the delivery yourself?" the sheriff asked.

"Yes. Are you surprised?"

"Well, I don't know. It seems strange—"

"To have a woman doing a man's work?"

The sheriff scratched his chin. "Let's say I woulda thought you'd be happier at home somewhere, married, than escorting a gold shipment for Ben Larrabee."

Lucy Roberts felt her face grow warm. "I can do most anything a man can, Sheriff. Ride, plow, shoe a horse.

# THEY DIDN'T TEACH THIS STUFF IN SCHOOL.

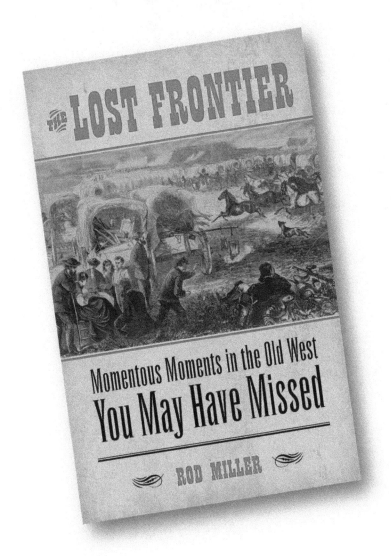

A lot of things happened in the Old West that didn't make it into the history books. Like the man who crossed North America years before Lewis and Clark. Or the man who flew an airplane decades before the Wright Brothers. Or the only man to rule America as Emperor. Read about these fascinating frontier figures and many more in the latest history book from Spur Award-winning author Rod Miller.

**The Lost Frontier: Momentous Moments in the Old West You May Have Missed** | ISBN: 978-1-4930-0735-6

www.writerRodMiller.com        T W O D O T®

# THE
# OKLAHOMANS

## The Story of Oklahoma and Its People

WILL ROGERS

**2017 GOLD MEDALIST**
BEST WESTERN NONFICTION

## Volume One: Ancient–Statehood

# JOHN J. DWYER

## FOREWORD BY GOVERNOR FRANK KEATING

w w w . j o h n j d w y e r . c o m

When I was little, on my pa's farm, I could kill a prairie dog with a rock at forty yards, every time."

"Well, the kind of varmints I'm thinking of are a sight bigger than prairie dogs, missy."

Lucy set her jaw and forced a deep breath.

"I should mention," she said, "that my wedding is next week, in Dodge. So I'll soon be home, and married. Does that please you, Sheriff?"

"Does it please you?" Charlie McCall said, from out of nowhere.

She blinked and looked at him. "What do you mean?"

The young man shrugged. He hadn't intended to be rude, she could see that—he just appeared curious. "The way you looked just then," he said, "you don't seem too happy about it."

She felt herself flush again. "I'm perfectly happy. Billy Ray Feeny is a fine man, and he'll make a fine husband. Not that it's any of your business."

McCall lifted his manacled hands. "My problem's none of your business, either," he said. "But it felt nice to know you're interested."

She regarded him for a long moment, feeling her anger drain away. She hadn't really been all that upset anyway: McCall's comment had been too close to the truth. She'd been having doubts about Billy Ray—and about her feelings for him—for weeks now. What bothered her even more, at this instant, were her feelings for this mysterious stranger. Even the sheriff seemed to realize something unusual was afoot here, as she and the young man stared into each other's eyes.

Suddenly the window darkened. For the moment, the rolling countryside was blocked from view; the stage had entered a small and scarce grove of trees. Just before they broke into the open again, something *THUMPED* on the roof of the coach. All three passengers looked up.

"One of the boxes tipped over, I expect," the sheriff said, as the stage began to slow down.

When they came to a full stop, he rose and stepped through the door. Lucy heard voices outside. Thirty seconds later the sheriff returned to the doorway, his face pale as chalk. "You two best come outside," he said.

The handcuffed man rose first, stepped down, then turned and helped Lucy down behind him. As soon as her feet touched ground she froze. Two men in tan dusters stood in the road near the front of the stagecoach, guns drawn and bandannas pulled tight over their lower faces. One of the men, tall and dark-haired, stayed close to the sheriff, whose own gun was missing from its holster. Three saddled horses were tied nearby.

"Line up right here, folks." The tall man waved his gunbarrel at the side of the stage. As they obeyed, Lucy noticed a third bandit, also masked. He wore a black hat and vest, and appeared to be unhitching the team from its traces.

The tall man—the leader, Lucy decided—was studying the three passengers. His gaze stopped on her. "We won't keep you long, Sheriff," he said, his eyes still fixed on Lucy. "All we want's the gold."

Lucy stiffened, which was apparently just what the tall man had been watching for. He looked at the second bandit and nodded. The second man climbed quickly past the driver's seat and onto the top of the stage. Lucy could hear him above and behind her as he rummaged through the bags and cases stored there. A minute later he stepped down again, carrying the banker's strongbox.

"Good," the leader said. "Tie it down and mount up." He then glanced at the bandit in the black vest, who was unhitching the last of the team. As everyone watched, Black Vest slapped the horse's rump and fired several shots into the air, sending all four horses thundering away into the hills north of the road. Within seconds they topped a rise and were gone.

"Where's our driver?" the sheriff asked. By now Lucy had figured out the noise they'd heard earlier—one of the thieves must have dropped from a tree limb onto the top of the coach. "I didn't hear a shot," he added.

The leader nodded to the east, the way the now-horseless stagecoach had come. "He got whacked on the head and fell off. He'll live, I imagine."

The sheriff's face hardened. "I'll find you, you know. Dodge City's no more'n twenty miles away. I can walk there by dark, and you'll be caught fore the week's out."

"Is that so," the tall man replied, amusement flickering in the eyes above his mask. Without saying more, he turned to Charlie McCall, and looked him up and down. The handcuffs were hard to miss. "Well, well. Seems we have a friend in the crowd."

McCall stared back at him.

THE RECKONING

AND OTHER STORIES OF THE WEST

DARREL

SPARKMAN

AUTHOR OF OSAGE DAWN

"Hold out your hands, boy," the tall man ordered, cocking his pistol.

McCall's hands were clasped together in front of him, the insides of his wrists resting on his belt. When he made no move to obey, the bandit raised his gun and thrust its muzzle against the handcuff's chain—and McCall's beltbuckle.

"You want my help or don't you?" the tall man asked.

"He can't hear you," Lucy said, alarmed.

The gunman ignored her. The two men looked into each other's eyes a moment, then McCall seemed to understand. He held his hands out to one side and stretched them apart. The gun roared, the chain separated. Still watching the leader's eyes, McCall rubbed his chafed wrists.

"Go," the leader said, with another wave of the gunbarrel. McCall gave him a final look, then turned and headed east, toward the grove of trees they had just passed through.

Once more, the tall man fixed his attention on the sheriff. The second bandit had secured the strongbox behind his horse's saddle and was mounted now, ready to leave. The third man—the one wearing the black vest—strolled over to the group and stood watching.

"You might walk out of here, sheriff," the leader said, "but not in half a day."

"What do you mean?" the lawman growled.

The leader nodded to Black Vest, who cocked his pistol and shot the toe off the sheriff's right boot. The big sheriff grunted once and fell heavily to the ground beside the stage. He lay still for a second or two, his eyes squeezed shut and both hands clutching his wounded foot. Though horrified, Lucy made no sound; she just knelt beside him and held him as he groaned through clenched teeth. She gave the black-vested man a glare of pure fury.

Without a word the bandit holstered his gun and backed away. The leader stepped forward and studied the fallen sheriff.

"That should slow you down a bit," he said. "I think a decent head start is only fair, don't you?" He glanced once at Lucy, then nodded to the others. The man with the gold spurred his horse south, and the leader swung into his saddle and followed. Black Vest stood where he was for a moment, watching Lucy and the sheriff with casual interest. He said, speaking for the first time, "Have a nice stroll, folks."

At the sound of his muffled voice, Lucy's narrowed eyes opened wide. Her face went slack.

"Billy Ray?" she said.

The black-vested gunman, who had already begun to turn away, froze where he stood. His eyes widened also, as he realized his mistake.

He and Lucy stared at each other for several long seconds. Finally he turned and almost ran to where his horse was tied. Behind him, Lucy rose unsteadily to her feet, pale with shock. He fumbled with untying the reins, and seemed to have trouble getting his foot in the stirrup. Once mounted, the bandit raced away in the direction his friends had gone.

He had covered only a short distance when Lucy's shout stopped him. Her face was flushed a fiery pink now, and she stood alone in the road twenty feet from the stage, one hand behind her back.

"Billy Ray!" she called.

He reined in, then wheeled his horse around so he could look back at her. He was between thirty and forty yards away.

She was ready. Her left arm was already extended, her right arm cocked back; in one smooth motion she snapped her upper body forward as hard as she could. The lemon-sized rock caught Billy Ray Feeny in the center of his forehead, and made a sound like an axe hitting the trunk of an oak. He flung both arms wide, opened his mouth in a perfect little O, and toppled backward out of the saddle. His riderless horse shied a step or two, then stopped.

Lucy watched the man fall and lie still. She was breathing hard, and barely heard Charlie McCall walk up behind her. He was half-carrying a dazed and bloodied old man she recognized as the stagecoach driver. Gently McCall propped the old-timer against one of the coach's wheels and gave the sheriff a glance. The big lawman had managed to get his boot off, and was tearing strips from his shirttail to use as bandages. Lucy blinked a few times, getting her bearings, then rushed to the sheriff to help him.

McCall said nothing to either of them. He started

walking south, moving neither slowly nor quickly, toward the spot where Billy Ray Feeny's horse stood grazing beside his sprawled form.

"Where's he going?" the sheriff said, his face pale and sweating.

"Let me do that," Lucy said, kneeling beside him.

"Where's he going? McCall?"

This time Lucy raised her head. Charlie McCall was still striding away, the broken handcuff chains swinging from his wrists.

"He's getting away," the sheriff murmured, half to himself. "He's getting away." He turned to her, his eyes wild. "Get my rifle. It's up top, in a brown pack."

"What?"

"Get it," he said, then shouted, *"McCallllll . . ."*

"He can't hear you," she said, staring after him, her mind whirling with a dozen disjointed thoughts.

Suddenly the sheriff pushed her away, and she sat down hard in the dirt. Muttering to himself, groaning with pain, he tried to hoist himself to his feet—

And then stopped. He was staring past her at McCall. She turned to look, and at first didn't understand what she was seeing.

Forty yards away, Charlie McCall had put on Billy Ray Feeny's black hat and vest and gunbelt and was mounting Feeny's horse. Without a single look back, he took off at a gallop, heading south across the rolling green hills.

"He's gone," the sheriff said, as if he found it impossible to believe. "He's gone with them."

Lucy stared into the distance until McCall had vanished from sight, then looked again at the sheriff. She didn't know what to think or believe anymore, after the events of the past twenty minutes. She could understand McCall's escape, and taking the gun, but why had he bothered with the hat and vest? He already had a hat.

She decided not to worry about it right now. What she did instead was help the sheriff scoot back into the shade of the coach and then tend to the gash on the old driver's head. After examining and cleaning the cut, she hurried to a gully she'd seen beside the road to get mud for a poultice for the sheriff's foot. Half an hour later both men were in considerably better shape, though she was half covered with dirt and blood and sweat.

And then, just as suddenly as he had left, Charlie

Pamela Foster

Award-Winning Author

www.pamela-foster.com

McCall rode into sight. He was leading a saddled horse and carrying two extra pistols in his belt. And on the extra horse was the strongbox of Ben Larrabee's gold.

He dismounted and tied both horses to the rear of the stage. "How's the foot?" he said.

The sheriff was speechless, and so, for the moment, was Lucy Roberts. She stared at McCall as if he were an apparition.

"What—what happened?" she asked, finally.

He tipped his hat back. "With the other guy's horse and clothes, I was able to get close enough to get the jump on 'em. They thought I was him." He pointed with his thumb. "I left them tied to a big oak beside a pond, about three miles south. They'll be okay till we ride into Dodge and get help." He added, with a disgusted look, "The other horse got away."

The sheriff was still gawking at him. "I—I thought—"

"I'm no criminal, Sheriff," McCall said. "I'll go with you, like before, but I'm no criminal."

The sheriff swallowed and nodded.

McCall turned then to Lucy, and their eyes held for what seemed a very long time. "There's one more thing to do," he said. "Get the rope off that saddle, would you?"

It took only a short while to drag Billy Ray Feeny's limp body back to the stage. He was still out cold, but he was alive, with a blue knot the size of a fist just above his eyes. "I saw you throw that rock," McCall said, when he finished tying the man's hands and feet. "Not bad."

"Well, he is a dog, and this is the prairie," she said. She managed to keep her tone light, but she was all too aware that this outlaw sprawled on the ground at her feet was the man who, until an hour ago, she had intended to marry. It was still a bit of a shock. She could see that the sheriff knew also. McCall, of course, didn't know. He had been down the road, attending to the driver, at the time she'd recognized Feeny, and of course couldn't have heard her call his name.

Lucy was also aware that she was at least partially responsible for this whole mess. She remembered now: Billy Ray Feeny had been in the bank, visiting with her,

when Mr. Larrabee asked her to escort the gold to Dodge City for him. It didn't take a genius to figure out the rest.

Even so, she was secretly grateful it had happened. She had not only discovered, and corrected, what had almost been the biggest mistake of her life—she had also met a man totally unlike anyone she had ever known before.

"You probably saved our lives," she said. "And my job, and my boss's gold."

McCall looked surprised. "You knocked the guy off his horse," he reminded her. "I couldn't have done anything without the horse."

"I guess we make a good team, then." She smiled, searching his eyes.

To her delight, he blushed a little. "I guess so," he said.

The plan, such as it was, didn't take long. She and Charlie McCall would ride into town on one horse and the driver on the other. The sheriff would stay here, in the shade of the stagecoach, with the still-unconscious prisoner, until they could return with the local law and

a doc. "Besides," the sheriff said, "I have to stay. If this guy wakes up I intend to shoot him in the foot."

Within ten minutes they were ready. With McCall's help, the stage driver was boosted onto the one horse, and he and Lucy climbed onto the other. Before leaving, while the sheriff was making himself comfortable and the driver had already started out down the road, McCall turned to Lucy and said to her, over his shoulder, "Guess you heard the sheriff say he'd speak for me? To the judge?"

She smiled and nodded. "He told me the charges were sure to be dropped."

McCall looked thoughtful. He didn't appear as happy about it as she thought he should be. "I suppose that means I'll soon be headed back home to Heritage, then," he said.

A silence passed. She just watched him, waiting.

"About your wedding . . ." He swallowed. "When's it supposed to be, exactly?"

She hesitated, studying his face. From the direction of the stage, the sheriff was humming a tune.

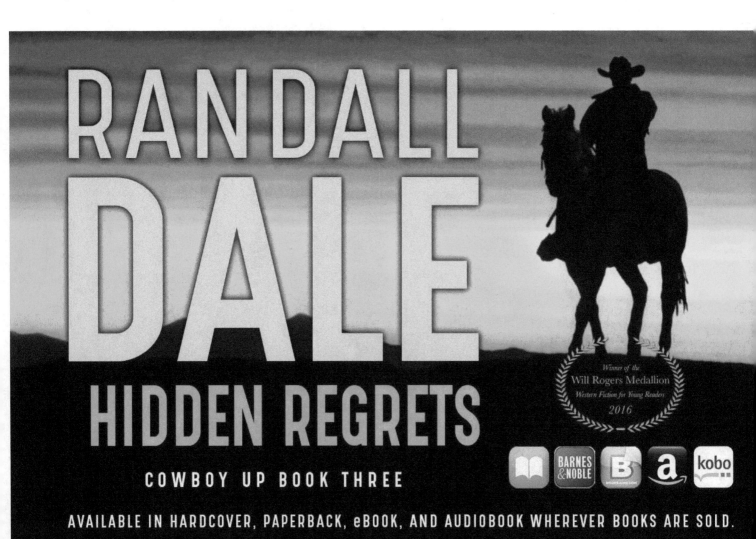

It occurred to her that Charlie McCall wasn't able to hear it.

Very carefully, making sure he was watching her lips, she answered, "The wedding's off."

He blinked. "What?"

"It's off. I'm not getting married."

"Ain't that kind of sudden?"

"You have no idea," she said, with a smile.

He frowned and cleared his throat. "Does that mean . . . Could that mean you'd come back home, too, then? To Heritage?"

Lucy felt a terrible weight on her heart. Just as she was about to speak, the driver called from up ahead, to see what the delay was. When she glanced ahead, past McCall's shoulder, he turned to follow her gaze.

"I'll have to stay in Dodge, Charlie," she answered, as he waved the old man on. "After all, my job's there."

But then she realized, as they faced each other again, that her words had gone unheard. He stared at her for a second, then asked, "Did I miss something?"

She swallowed. "I answered your question.".

But then something happened. The look in his eyes, at that moment, was so intense, so full of concern and expectation and emotion, it made her skin tingle. Suddenly the weight lifted, and Lucy knew for certain what this strange feeling in her heart was. She knew it as surely as she knew her own name. Out here in the middle of nowhere, sitting on a horse that had belonged to a man she thought she had known but hadn't known at all, sitting behind a man she had only just met, she realized she had finally found her gold, and it wasn't the kind you buy or steal or put in a strongbox.

"Would you care to repeat it?" McCall asked. He looked as if he might be holding his breath.

She reached up and brushed a wisp of hair off his forehead. "What I said was—I won't be staying in Dodge after all. I'm coming back home, to Heritage."

Very slowly, both of them grinned.

Up ahead, the old-timer was staring at them, waiting. McCall glanced at him, then turned again to Lucy.

"Guess it's time to go," he said, still smiling.

"Well, let's go then. You're driving."

# JOHN M. FLOYD

John M. Floyd's work has appeared in more than 250 different publications, including *Alfred Hitchcock's Mystery Magazine, Ellery Queen's Mystery Magazine, The Strand Magazine, Woman's World, The Saturday Evening Post,* and *The Best American Mystery Stories.* A former Air Force captain and IBM systems engineer, John is also an Edgar Award nominee, a three-time Derringer Award winner, a three-time Pushcart Prize nominee, and the recipient of the Edward D. Hoch Memorial Golden Derringer Award for lifetime achievement. John published his first book, *Rainbow's End,* in 2006, followed by *Midnight* (2008), *Clockwork* (2010), *Deception* (2013), *Fifty Mysteries* (2014), and *Dreamland* (2016). His seventh book, *The Barrens,* is scheduled for release in fall 2018. He can be found online at **www.johnmfloyd.com.**

"Lucy's Gold" is John's first story to appear in the pages of *Saddlebag Dispatches.*

# DUSTY RICHARDS

# STEALING TIME

## FROM "DUMB AS A NEWBORN DUCK" TO WESTERN WRITING LEGEND

*STORY BY*

### CYNDY PRASSE MILLER

*PHOTOS BY*

### JOHNNY D. BOGGS

### CASEY W. COWAN • KELLY D. WILLIS

Many people, including myself, have called Dusty Richards a legend. But what does that mean? How does one define *legend?* Webster's Dictionary describes a legend as "a story coming down from the past, regarded as historical but not verifiable." Another usage is "a person or thing that inspires." Both definitions can be applied to Dusty Richards, but those descriptions only begin to touch the tip of the iceberg. There is so much more to the legend. Where does one begin?

American football player J.J. Watt is quoted as saying, "If you want to be remembered as great, if you want to be a legend, you have to go out there every single day and do stuff." Anybody who ever met Dusty Richards would say that he never aspired to be great, to be a legend— but nobody would dispute that he went out there every single day and did stuff. Dusty and his wife Pat were constantly researching material for his next book, attending writer's events, mingling with community members, and spending time with their families. Whatever the activity was, Dusty gave it all his attention and effort. He was larger than life, and his energy carried bystanders along with him.

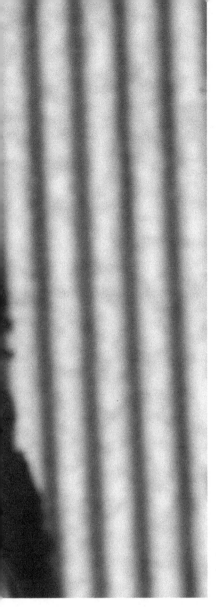

If the key to becoming a legend doesn't hinge on the desire to do so, then how does one become a legend? Is it through hard work? Many people are hard workers, yet no one knows their name. Is it through building a legacy by mentoring and teaching others? Many great teachers have influenced hundreds yet are remembered by few. Are legends created when a person with vast wealth gives heavily to charities or is this an act that is expected from the wealthy? Is the key to do good works in the community? That is helpful of course, but unless a building bears your name, few will remember the deeds when you are gone.

How, then, is a legend created? What is the significant difference between an ordinary man, and one who is known far and wide for generations to come? What is it about one man that sets him apart from all others?

If we are going to attempt to answer that question, we need to get to know Dusty better, to know where he came from and where he traveled along life's journey to become the person we knew. We need to follow him as he became a cowboy, a rancher, a chicken doctor, a media personality, and an author who *True West* magazine called "the greatest western fiction writer alive." We need to see inside his mind and his heart, to understand what made him different from, and the same as, those surrounding him.

When one thinks of cowboys, visions of the Wild West, or at least the western United States, come to mind. Men born in a dusty land, surrounded by sagebrush, horses, and cattle, sitting around campfires, drinking coffee and swapping stories after a hard day's ride. Families trying to scratch out a living in a hostile land, good guys in white hats fighting to protect the innocent. This is the world that Dusty Richards brought to life for his readers, but ironically it was not the world he was born into.

The United States in 1937 was a mixture of triumphs and tragedies. Unemployment continued to drop as the country

fought back from the Great Depression. Amelia Earhart was lost somewhere over the Pacific Ocean. The Golden Gate Bridge opened in San Francisco, becoming the longest suspension bridge in the world at that time. The German airship *Hindenburg* crashed. Americans were introduced to *Daffy Duck, Snow White and the Seven Dwarves,* and actor and future President Ronald Reagan. In Chicago, the first United States blood bank opened and the Memorial Day Massacre occured, leaving ten union demonstrators dead.

On Thursday, November 11, 1937, Ronald Lee Richards was born in Chicago, the oldest child of John and Jean Hogenbirk Richards. John Richards was a stationary power plant engineer, and Jean was a homemaker, raising Ronald and his brother and sister in the family's rented home. His family moved around when Ronald was young, allowing him to experience his first taste of the cowboy life. He went to a roundup in Washington state when he was just seven years old, sat on a real horse and watched the cowboys brand the calves. If there was a Saturday movie matinee featuring his heroes Hoppy, Roy, or Gene, he was there.

At that time, people didn't worry as much about the age of someone they hired, and Dusty's family had instilled a strong work ethic into him. He always had a job, beginning at an early age—delivering groceries, selling extra produce from his grandmother's garden, raising rabbits and chickens, mowing lawns, helping with polo ponies, even working in a sale barn.

When Ronald was thirteen, his family moved to Arizona—first to Mesa, and then a year later to Phoenix. When they moved to Phoenix, Ronald told everyone that his name was "Dusty", and it stuck with him the rest of his life.

In Arizona, he went to work on a farm—milking cows, feeding hogs, harvesting citrus fruits from the trees. In the wintertime, he helped run cattle in the cotton fields while fattening them on culled lettuce and carrots. Soon he had a horse of his own to ride. With ranches to work on, rodeos to ride in, cowboys to learn from, the family's move to Arizona placed Dusty squarely in his own heaven.

A local rancher named Joe Chavez hired him to go on a roundup, where everyone except Dusty spoke Spanish. They laughed at him when he tried to string

"IF YOU WANT TO BE A WRITER, YOU **HAVE TO WRITE**. **EVERY DAY**.
SOMETIMES YOU WON'T FEEL LIKE IT, BUT YOU MUST. YOU WILL
NEVER HAVE THE TIME TO BE A WRITER, **YOU MUST STEAL THE TIME**.
YOU HAVE TO MAKE THE **COMMITMENT TO YOUR WRITING**."

Spanish words together, calling him the little gringo. At age thirteen, he gained the very real experiences of a nose full of smoke from the branding irons, and the bloody mess of castration and de-horning.

With the move to Phoenix, Dusty approached the Milky Way Hereford Ranch for employment. The Milky Way was known for its premium bulls, some worth as much as $100,000. Remember, this was the 1950s. While Dusty got the job, paying fifty cents an hour, he wasn't allowed to start out working with the cattle. His first chore on the ranch was taking a bucket of poison out to the fields to kill off the red ants. He eventually moved up to washing the bulls and was driving the cattle around in the ton-and-a-half ranch truck by the time he was fifteen.

Working on ranches and participating in cattle roundups landed Dusty several bit parts in television and movie Westerns as well. He rode in posses in the *Zane Grey Theater,* was in *Wanted Dead or Alive* with Steve McQueen, was on the set of *Rio Bravo,* and managed to be in several episodes of *Gunsmoke.* Dusty even scored an appearance with Marilyn Monroe in the film *Bus Stop.*

Always a voracious reader, Dusty found time between school and work to read every Western novel he could get his hands on at the library, and by the time he got to high school he had progressed to buying paperbacks. He said they "cost a quarter and lined the racks at the drugstores by the zillions." When he couldn't buy books, he wrote his own. He began his career as a writer by writing book reports on nonexistent Western books and selling the reports to "other boys too lazy to read," because "English teachers never read Westerns," and didn't know the reports were made up. At that time, teenagers were lucky to earn fifty cents an hour, and the money he made kept him and his friends in gas money to go back and forth to school.

Although Dusty loved the rodeos, his

DUSTY **SPEAKS OUT** DURING A WESTERN WRITERS OF AMERICA **BOARD MEETING** IN KANSAS CITY IN JUNE, 2017.

destiny wasn't to be a rodeo cowboy, but an announcer. Looking for a way to make money, he signed up to ride bulls in a small rodeo in the town of Chandler, Arizona. The man who handled the rodeo stock told Dusty to go upstairs and announce the rodeo. Dusty replied he wasn't an announcer, to which the man retorted, "You sure ain't a bull rider either." The job paid $25, and Dusty didn't have to get thrown in the dirt by a bull.

His mother's greatest fear was that her son would never achieve anything and be a "cowboy bum." After graduating from Phoenix High School in 1955, he attended Arizona State University, graduating in 1960 with a bachelor of science degree in agriculture.

At age twenty-three, a degree in hand, Dusty headed east, along with two of his best friends. Together they bought seven hundred and thirteen acres, for a price of around $13,000— "a worn out, overgrown patch in the Boston Mountains" west of Winslow, Arkansas. While getting the ranch up and running, Dusty taught high school science and biology in the nearby towns of Winslow and Huntsville during the 1961-62 school year. It was during this time that he met beautiful young Pat Donahoe, who became his lifelong bride on June 5, 1961. True to his earlier work ethic, Dusty did anything and everything he could to keep the ranch running and provide for his new bride and the two daughters they would soon have.

In 1963, Dusty landed a job with Tyson Feed and Hatchery, later named Tyson Foods, starting with them "three days before President Kennedy was shot." While working for the Tyson company for more than three decades, most of the time spent in a supervisory position, he managed to find time for ranching and other business pursuits. He served as Justice of the Peace, sold real estate, became a licensed auctioneer, and a rodeo announcer.

Dusty and Pat were always active

**DUSTY CELEBRATES** HIS **THIRD SPUR AWARD WIN** WITH LONGTIME FRIEND AND FELLOW AUTHOR **JODI THOMAS** IN JUNE, 2017.

THE RANCH BOSS. HERE AT **SADDLEBAG DISPATCHES**, THAT WAS NOT ONLY HIS NICKNAME, BUT HOW WE THOUGHT OF HIM—**THE MASTER STORYTELLER, THE ICON, THE LIVING LEGEND. THERE WILL NEVER BE ANOTHER DUSTY.**

members of the community, and this outgoing spirit led Dusty to pursue roles in the public eye. He conducted a live radio farm report from 6 a.m. to 7 a.m. on KFAY-AM in Fayetteville every weekday for thirteen years, anchored a morning television news program in Fort Smith and Fayetteville for seven years, and wrote a humor column for a weekly newspaper.

He did all of this while raising a family and writing his stories, always harboring a dream of writing Western novels. Dusty often told the story about sitting on the porch of the dilapidated cabin on Mrs. Winter's ranch

couldn't figure out what was missing from those stories. When his daughters were teenagers, they found his stories and encouraged him to sell them. Dusty stepped into the world of publishing, in his own words "dumb as a newborn duck." He managed to sell three books to a small printer in Missouri, but after two years without seeing his books in print, he severed the tie with that company. Twenty years later, he discovered that the books had indeed been printed, without his knowledge, but he was never able to find and buy copies for himself.

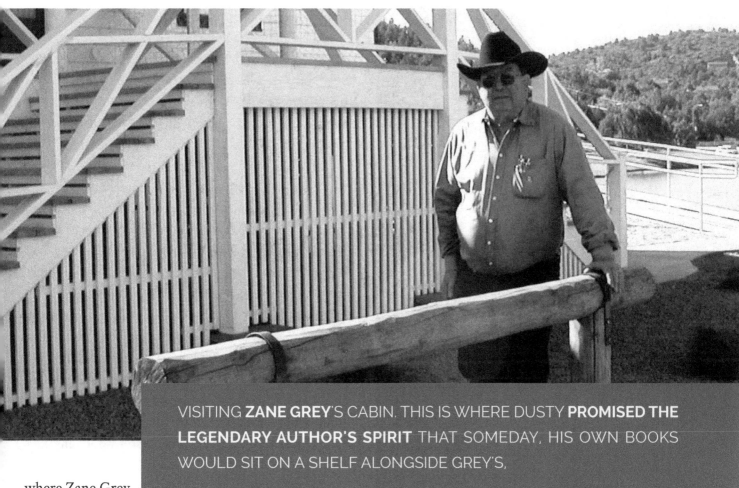

VISITING **ZANE GREY**'S CABIN. THIS IS WHERE DUSTY **PROMISED THE LEGENDARY AUTHOR'S SPIRIT** THAT SOMEDAY, HIS OWN BOOKS WOULD SIT ON A SHELF ALONGSIDE GREY'S,

where Zane Grey wrote his novels. He thought of Grey writing his books in longhand, in a loose-leaf notebook. Dusty vowed to the author's ghost that someday he would have his books on the shelves alongside Grey's.

Beginning with those early book reports, Dusty never completely stopped writing. He wrote his stories in longhand in notebooks. He wrote and wrote, always knowing his stories didn't have that special something that made stories sell. But he

Dusty credited the beginning of his real success as a writer to Dr. Frank Reuter, retired teacher and editor. He was introduced to Reuter at the Ozarks Writers League conference in Branson, Missouri in 1985. By this time, he had already written a lot of books, and feeling that Reuter's prices for editing were reasonable, he sent him a book that, in his mind, was polished and ready for publication. He recalls that "the red ink could have kept the blood bank supplied all summer." There

were notes all over the pages, between the lines, and on the back. The second book came back with some pages that weren't marked on at all. After editing the third book, Reuter told Dusty that he may not have edited it as hard because he was too busy reading it. In Dusty's mind, that compliment was the sign that the book would sell.

The same day that he met Dr. Reuter, Jory Sherman handed Dusty a membership application for Western Writers of America. His application was accepted, and Dusty credited Jory Sherman with being a good guide for him, helping him learn about agents and the publishing business.

Although he had written many books through the years and was beginning to learn the business and have small successes, his big break came with the publication of *Noble's Way*, the same manuscript that Reuter had been "busy reading." The manuscript had been rejected by St. Martin's Press, as it didn't quite fit what they were looking for. The rejection letter contained a statement that M. Evans, another publishing company "needs this book." So, Dusty bundled up his manuscript, along with his cover letter and the rejection letter from St. Martin's Press. In his words, "I figured if they needed it, they needed to know they needed it." M. Evans must have agreed—they published the novel in 1992.

Dusty recalls that he committed to a career as a writer after having a good friend pass away at a relatively young age. He knew that his friend had big plans for when he retired and that those plans would never be fulfilled now. Realizing that the future holds no guarantees, he talked to Pat, and it was decided that Dusty would retire from Tyson Foods in 1994 and dedicate himself to writing full-time.

Dusty's approach to writing was to get in the saddle and ride down the trail, telling the best story he could along the way. He never used a roadmap for his stories, and any outline he had was kept in his head, subject to change at the whim of the characters. His extensive experience as a cowboy and rancher, along with constant research, permits the characters to achieve an authenticity not seen in other novels. He allowed his characters to tell their stories, going in directions that he hadn't originally planned on taking them.

He studied people in the everyday world, noting

speech patterns, phrases, gestures, facial expressions, the way they walked, troubles and triumphs they were telling their friends. Anybody he met ran the risk of ending up as a character in one of his novels. This made the characters more real, more relatable for the readers.

To produce believable narratives, Dusty read history, found old newspaper accounts of what he wanted to know about, studied the diaries of people from the time period, and learned what life was really like for the people who settled the West.

Whenever possible, Dusty and Pat would visit the places he was writing about to gain a better understanding of the setting, as well as conduct local research. He studied the seasons, the time of day, the plants and animals of the area, the lay of the land. All of this helped create authentic backgrounds for the characters he created.

And what amazing characters he created! These fictional people represented everything Dusty loved about the West, brought to the page bigger than life. The "good" guys were men of vision, brought to this wild land by destiny. The "bad" guys were full of greed and selfishness, hiding behind the façade of average citizens. All the people he wrote about were full of "grit and determination." The government had seized land from the Indians and given it away to the settlers in land rushes. The land they went to homestead was poor ground, land that should never have been farmed, "but by the time they found that out, they had either starved to death or moved on."

The less daring people, the meek and the weak, stayed behind in the cities, content to work in factories and die early deaths from pollution and bad food, poisoned with fumes and the preservatives that were being added to their meals to prevent spoilage. The courageous and strong headed west, determined to make a better life for themselves and their families, to live with clean air and water, and grow their own food. To carve out their future on their own terms. These are the people Dusty Richards grew up around, the people that made him determined to be a cowboy, to be a writer and memorialize them in his novels. These are the people who populated the more than 150 books he wrote, plus innumerable articles and short stories.

Some of you might be thinking, "He was retired.

Of course, he had plenty of time to write." Have I mentioned Dusty's strong work ethic? His commitment to his family and his community? Because in addition to writing full-time, Dusty Richards served on the board of Ozarks Electric Corporation in Arkansas, and the statewide board for rural electric in Oklahoma, was a board member for Ozark Creative Writers Conference,

Dusty spent countless hours helping other writers become the best writers they could be. He never criticized anyone's stories, always offered encouragement. He taught by focusing on the positives in the writing, always telling the author, "The important thing is to get the story out and write it down. Any problems there are, you can fix those later. For now, just get the story down." When he

POSING WITH **BIGFOOT** IN FAYETTEVILLE, ARKANSAS, SPRING, 2014.

Ozark Writers League, Oklahoma Writers Federation, Springdale PRCA rodeo, past President of Western Writers of America, President of Northwest Arkansas Writers. He mentored hundreds of other writers, attended events where he lectured on writing techniques, taught others to navigate the publishing business, and attended conferences to learn more and hone his craft.

was handed a manuscript or heard a writer read a story aloud, he always responded with positive comments, along the lines of "That's a good story. There are a few problems, but we can fix those." For Dusty, it was always about the joy of creating a story for the readers. He stated that "editing is drudgery, writing a synopsis is boring." Those are things that need to be done but was never where the joy was found.

Dusty never forgot the hard road that he took to become a writer and wanted to help others avoid the pitfalls. He said it took him ten years to be accepted as a writer. That is a long time for a writer to struggle, but "six months is ten minutes in an editor's life." He stressed to new writers to be patient and not give up. Dr. Frank Reuter, his editor and teacher, told him that

Between novels, he would write short stories. He considered short stories to be "the best thing to practice on. You get results quickly and you learn to be sparse with words."

Some of the people who came to him for advice, he couldn't help. Not because he wasn't willing, but because they were only looking for praise. They didn't want to hear him tell them what they must do

DUSTY WAS ALWAYS **PASSIONATE** ABOUT **HELPING** HIS **FELLOW WRITERS**. HERE HE POSES WITH OTHER MEMBERS OF THE OGHMA CREATIVE MEDIA FAMILY: (LEFT TO RIGHT): GIL MILLER, VELDA BROTHERTON, VIVIAN CUMMINGS, PETER JEPPSEN, ALICE CAI, AND VENESSA CERASALE.

he had met many writers that he thought would do well, but they had given up. The most determined man that Frank Reuter knew was Dusty Richards. Dusty wrote good stories, but his tenacity was what eventually brought success.

He never took no for an answer, just kept writing.

to be successful, so they didn't listen. "I could help the students that wanted to listen and learn, the student who reads. If you don't read, don't expect to become a writer."

People always wanted to know how he managed

to write so many stories, and still maintain his busy schedule of other commitments. He credited his wife Pat for his success, for encouraging him every day. He would come home from work when he was still working for Tyson and write "from six until ten. At ten my wife would come get me to watch the news with her."

Everywhere he went, Dusty gave advice to aspiring writers. "If you want to be a writer, you have to write. Every day. Sometimes you won't feel like it, but you must. You will never have the time to be a writer, you must steal the time. You have to make the commitment to your writing."

When asked how to become a good writer, he responded "Practice your writing. Sometimes what you write won't be any good. But that is how you get better. Read other writers and learn from them. Don't copy them but learn how they write. Then use that. When you have more experience, your writing will be better. Don't worry if it is good enough or not, just write the entire first draft. Then you will have your story, and you will be committed to editing it and making it a book."

When he finished the draft, he would "leave the computer with hard copies, double-spaced, and tear it apart, add, subtract, and read it again. He'd scribble with pencil, mark on it with a highlighter, go back to the computer for the next draft, print out new hard copies and do it all again—and again, until it was good enough to send to the publisher."

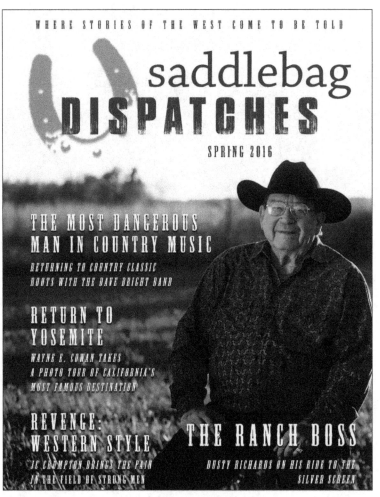

The years of struggle to become a published writer, the hours spent writing the stories and editing, the time spent helping other writers, and in turn, improving his own writing finally began to pay off in big ways. His books were selling, and Dusty was beginning to be recognized across the country as a serious writer of traditional western novels.

In both 2003 and 2004, Dusty was given the award for Best Fiction Book of the Year from the Oklahoma Writer's Federation. In 2004, he was inducted into the Arkansas Writers Hall of Fame. 2007 saw him win two Spur Awards from Western Writers of America. The Cowboy Hall of Fame in Oklahoma City presented him with the Wrangler Award in 2009. He earned the Will Rogers Medallion in 2010, and again in 2016.

But Dusty wasn't satisfied yet. Dusty dreamed of creating a magazine, one that would keep the spirit of the West alive, stories that would honor those who represented the tough men and women who settled this country, as well as the native people who were already here. Stories of the Old West, the new West, of cowboys and horses and pickup trucks. Stories of the lives of Native Americans, then and now. A magazine whose motto is "A Place Where Stories of the West Come to be Told." This was the kind of magazine that Dusty Richards wanted to help create, and in the autumn of 2014, in conjunction with Oghma Creative Media, that dream became a reality with the first issue of *Saddlebag Dispatches*.

"I ONCE GOT A LETTER FROM **A SOLDIER'S WIFE**, A CANADIAN SOLDIER. SHE SAID HER **HUSBAND WAS MY BIGGEST FAN** AND WANTED TO SEE ABOUT GETTING AN AUTOGRAPH FOR HIM. HE WAS **FIGHTING OVER IN AFGHANISTAN** THEN. I SENT HIM FOUR OF MY BOOKS, AND **THANKED HIM** FOR BEING OVER THERE."

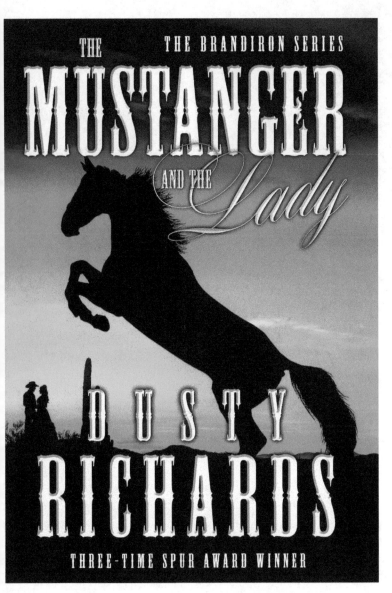

With over 100 books to his credit, worldwide recognition as a Western novelist, numerous awards and honors, and now a magazine—what did Dusty have left to prove? Well into his seventies, wasn't it time to retire and take it easy, maybe indulge more in trout fishing, one of his favorite pastimes? But no, that wasn't his nature. Dusty lived every day to the fullest. Besides, he still had stories to tell, books to write.

When asked if there was anything he would still like to see happen with his writing, he replied, "I'd like to see one of my books become a movie. I'd like people who don't read a lot to know about these stories too. That would be great. I've heard people say that movies ruin the books, but I think that if it gets someone to know about your book, that's okay. Everyone is going to have a different take on the story anyway."

As the world changed and the internet took hold, readers no longer looked only to bookstores and libraries to find their reading material. Online bookstores, electronic books, and audiobooks became more popular than ever before. Recommendations for readers appeared through email, online advertising, and social media. Although Dusty's genre was the traditional western, as an author he moved right along with the times. He always understood the importance of coming to where the fans were, of being accommodating to the changing world.

Even though he was willing to use the power of the internet to reach more readers, as well as other writers, he stayed realistic about the way the internet, and especially social media, could help writers. "I think writers need to worry first about having a good product. Those e-books with typos, grammatical errors, stupid dialogue, and no plot… if you sell junk, the reader is left with a bad taste in their mouth and won't give you another try. Concentrate on improving your writing skills and writing more books to have something to sell. I know people who spend all their time on Facebook and Twitter when they should be writing, or trying to do book signings all the time. I do signings when they're convenient, I get exposure and get to meet the fans. The few books you sell at signings won't earn your gas money back. But I still do them. I just don't let all that interfere with the writing."

In 2016, Dusty Richards published his 150th western novel, *The Mustanger and the Lady*. By any standards, this was an amazing achievement, but remember, he didn't publish his first novel until 1992. That is an average of more than six published books a year, in addition to his commitments to family and community.

The next year, Western Writers of America awarded him a third Spur award for *The Mustanger and the Lady*, a book that was already being adapted for film. In the fall of 2017, weeks before Dusty's 80th birthday, the film *Painted Woman* was released in theaters. Dusty and Pat traveled to venues around Arkansas and Oklahoma, attending as many of the premieres as they could, shaking hands and meeting fans. For them, the book sales and awards were great, but it was the fans that he was the proudest of, the reason he kept putting those stories out there.

While Dusty was celebrating the success of having one of his books made into a film, he began planning another project. A story of a cowboy who was bigger than life, a man who stayed humble when others called him a legend, a cowboy born in Chicago—the story of Dusty Richards. Fate stepped in before that project was finished and pulled Dusty and Pat up to that big campfire in the sky. We are sure Dusty is sitting up there, swapping stories with the writers and cowboys he admired, and Pat is sitting to the side reading a romance, shaking her head at his tall tales. But even now, Dusty still has stories to tell here on Earth. The manuscripts he left behind will continue to be published for years to come.

Jazz Musician Miles Davis was once quoted as saying, "A legend is an old man with a cane known for what he used to do. I'm still doing it." Dusty Richards is known for what he used to do—write Westerns, mentor writers, guide and encourage community members, be an example for family and friends. But with all he left behind, he can say that he is still doing all those things. His physical presence will be missed by those who knew him. But the essence of Dusty Richards will live on through every life he touched.

*That* is the stuff that legends are made of.

*—Cyndy Prasse Miller has been a waitress, factory worker, wood carver, personal assistant, office drone, and archaeologist. After spending years studying people and cultures, both living and non-living, she is now pursuing a career writing their stories. She and her husband, a fellow author and bibliophile, make their home in the Ozarks, where she predicts they will meet their deaths under a collapsing bookcase.*

STEF **DAWSON**    DAVID THOMAS **JENKINS**
KIOWA **GORDON** WITH MATT **DALLAS**
AND ROBERT **CRAIGHEAD**

# PAINTED WOMAN

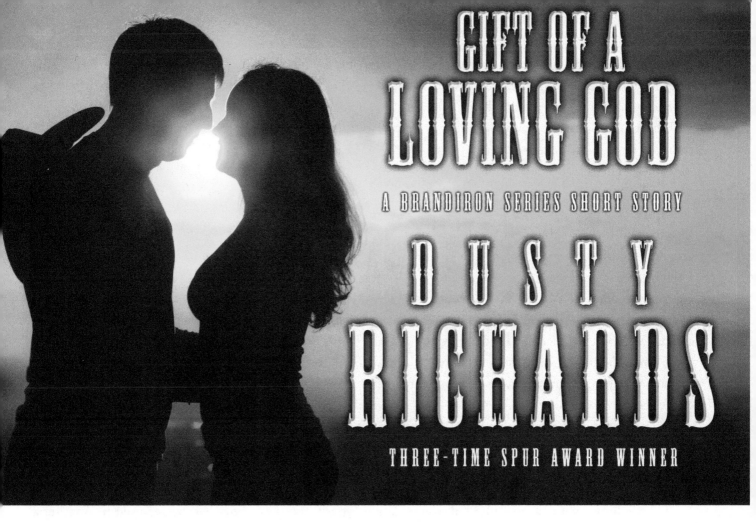

# GIFT OF A LOVING GOD

## A BRANDIRON SERIES SHORT STORY

# DUSTY RICHARDS

### THREE-TIME SPUR AWARD WINNER

Things were in a hellacious uproar across southeast Arizona and southwest New Mexico. The U.S. Army and Army scouts had been charging all over after renegade Apaches. Most folks had brought their families in from their ranches to the small towns in the area under the threat of more Apache attacks. Others set up fortifications at their home ranches and were armed to the teeth to withstand any attacks.

Burl Waller had gone into Tombstone for supplies and was headed back to his ranch with a swift team of horses hitched on his buckboard. No grass was growing under those ponies' hooves when he rounded a corner and about ran over a prone body in the road. His quick action avoided hitting the figure on the ground and he stood up and hauled the lathered team to a stop.

Who was it? He wrapped up his reins, drew his Colt .44, just in case, and jumped down to see if they were even alive. He found the person was wrapped in a blanket and when he turned her over, he discovered she was a young, pale-faced, unconscious woman. With the hair on the back of his neck standing up, he

looked over the chaparral country. Nothing moved or showed themselves. He holstered his handgun, swept her up and put her in the back between his supplies.

Who was she? She had no blood on her, nor did she look beat up. How did she get out there? She didn't wake up during his transfer. Maybe at Childers's Crossing someone would know where she belonged. He was back on the spring seat wondering who, why, and where as he slapped the horses on their rumps and sent them southeast.

Occasionally, he looked back over his shoulder at her still form. There was not a sign of consciousness in her. She had been breathing and not with much trouble. But he'd be at Childers's shortly and maybe someone there could answer his questions.

He topped the next hill and saw the smoke. That was something on fire. Childers's had a small store with a saloon at the crossroads between Tombstone and the road to Fort Huachuca. That store ahead must be burning. Damn those redskin bastards, anyway. The raiders would be gone by the time he got there. The tall streak of smoke would draw any army outfit in the desert there immediately.

He stood up and his passenger wrapped in the blanket between his supplies had not moved. He hoped she hadn't died. Nothing he could do but drive on.

Burl took a shortcut toward his place, risking running head-on into a band of Apaches out in the brush. The greasewood rubbed his spokes and the smell of creosote was powerful. He crossed the sandy dry wash and could see the ranch and corrals. He swept into the yard and the two Mexican boys, Ornaldo and Micah, came from the house armed with Winchesters.

"Ah, you made it." Micah said. "Who is that?"

"We better get her inside. Help me get her out. Be careful, she's unconscious. I found her lying on the road. Open the door." He hoisted her into his arms. He carried her in to put her on his bed in the middle of the room.

Her blue eyes flew open in shock. "Who are you?"

"Burl Waller. Who are you?"

"I'm sorry. I'm not sure." She looked like she was in shock at the fact that she couldn't spit out her name.

"I don't know your story, lady, but you're safe here. These boys and me are armed to the teeth. This old rock house is a fort. It has a tin roof, so fire arrows won't burn it down. But we're ready. Now you rest, and your past will catch up with you."

"I am very grateful for you seeing about me. My mind is very confused." She fell back on the pillow and held the back of her hand to her forehead. "Why can't I tell you who I am?"

He folded his arms. "I repeat, you're safe here. Don't fret, things will return to you. The more you worry, the more you lock them out. The boys and I aren't great cooks, but we will fix something to eat. I bet you've missed some meals.

"I don't even know that."

"Rest."

"I'll try."

He turned to his two helpers. "Any Indians come around while I was in town?"

"No," Ornaldo said. He was eighteen and a good hand with a gun, rope, or horse.

Micah, his shorter cousin, was sixteen and a smart youth, too. Both boys had been raised in Apacheria

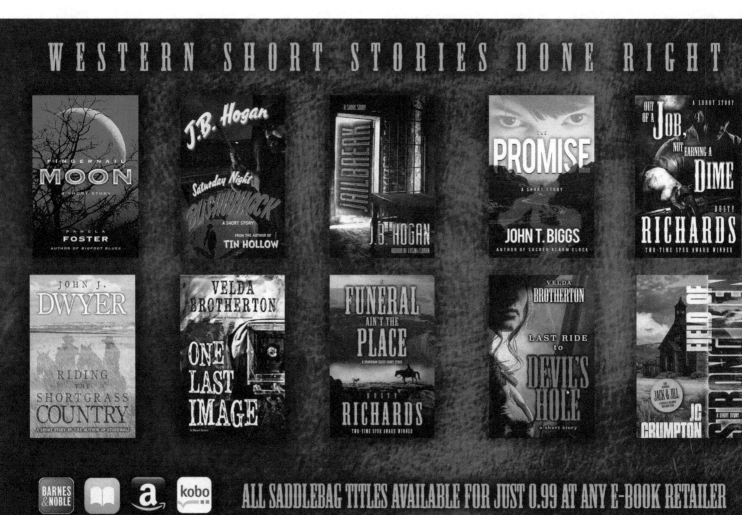

and they knew the threat well. They had lost family members in raids on the village where they were raised south of the border. Help was short. The high-paying mines in Tombstone got the miners. Not many cowboys looking for work ventured into the region because of the Apaches. He and his boys ran his ranch and used the good local beef market to make a profit on his operation.

Soon they had some *frijoles* cooking on the wood-burning stove. Burl also started to boil some oatmeal, thinking it might be more kind to their guest's stomach. Besides, the beans would require hours to be boiled tender.

When next he glanced over at their patient, she had slipped off into sleep. Good, maybe rest would restore her mind. He hoped so. She was someone's wife, daughter—whatever. She was nice enough looking and her clothes were not rags. That spoke of some wealth, at least. Too nice a female, anyway, for a crusty thirty-two-year-old rancher who'd been a bachelor all his life.

He'd come out of Texas after the war. Found this ranch and had enough money of his own from cattle drives to Kansas to buy the Three L. He wondered if he'd known then the full threat of Apaches, would he ever have bought there. But he had to make it work or turn up his toes. The beef market in Tombstone was a good one, so he'd stayed. This would be his third year in the territory. He bought stocker cattle in Mexico, drove them up and ranged them in his wide valley's grass until they fattened. He and his two hands made the deal work.

With his palm, he scrubbed the two weeks beard stubble on his face, something that hadn't bothered him until he got in her company. Oh, she'd soon be back where she belonged and never worry a minute about his shaggy looks or the dusty six-foot tall cowboy that found her lying in the road.

He felt guilty having this woman on his hands with three men and her cooped up in a small *jacal.* She was very modest, but she didn't know her name for anything. That frustrated her, but she never complained. They came to call her Jane. Soon, she did the cooking and they enjoyed an improved diet.

Some troopers came by to check on them and said, they thought the Apache renegades had gone back to the Sierra Madres in Mexico. They knew nothing of the woman or where she came from, so, he planned to take Jane to Tombstone in the morning. They had a nice arm's length relationship, but he never was much of a ladies' man. She acted very reserved and demure, not like some ladies of the night he occasionally visited in one of the sporting houses in Tombstone.

He cleaned up and put on his white shirt, tie, and coat. They let her have the *casa* after they brought her heated bath water. She thanked them. When she was ready he helped her on the buckboard seat and they drove off to Tombstone.

His first stop was the courthouse. None of Sheriff Behan's deputies recognized her. They acted like he should leave her there with someone until her people came looking for her since she had no knowledge of who she was. That was not what he planned, short of finding her people. He checked with several people and left a notice to be printed in both newspapers that a young woman had been found and due to her lack of memory needed to be identified.

When he left the last newspaper office, she put her hand on his knee on the buckboard and spoke quite frankly. "I'm afraid someone will say, 'she is mine' and not be telling the truth and I'd have to go with them, Burl."

"Only answer for that is for me to buy a marriage license and marry you."

"Oh, you don't have to do that." They were stopped in his buckboard about to block traffic.

"If your real man came, I'd apologize and give you back. That way they couldn't take you like you're talking about."

"I don't want to be a burden."

"Would you marry me?"

She nodded and acted relieved.

"Good enough. Let's do it."

He turned the rig around in the middle of the block and went back to the courthouse. Getting a marriage license for Jane Doe was not easy but they got one and were married. He kissed the bride and they went by the doctor's office.

Doc Farley rung out his left ear a few times with his index finger, after checking her. He explained she might slow-like regain her past memory. No doubt she had suffered a severe blow to the head and had no idea when that happened. He said she was extremely healthy and then in a whisper said she had been married sometime in the past he was confident.

Burl never took that note as anything but part of her past life they didn't know about. She looked at him concerned over the matter and he dismissed it. "We don't know how that went, is all I can say, Jane."

She agreed with his confidence and they thanked the doctor and went out to the buckboard. He stopped her to talk before they got on the rig.

"Now, I'm not pushing you into anything you don't want to do. We are married and legal like, unless—"

Her finger on his lips silenced him. "I know what you're going to say. I haven't any but you, Burl. If I had someone, they surely would have come looking for me by now. I'm your wife and I'm happy to be so. I *want* to be."

"Girl, that solves all my problems. I'm getting us a hotel room, and you'll be my wife sure enough."

She stood on her toes and kissed his cheek. "You have treated me so nice. Thank you, sir."

That spot she kissed on his shaven face burned like a hot branding iron. He got them a back room on the second floor of the Alhambra Hotel, a quieter place than the ones on the street side, and they had a honeymoon. He never regretted a second of it. For him it was like some religious ceremony to have a wife to love him.

He found her beauty and her pleasing ways toward him as some great gift from a generous God. Nothing he even deserved had been handed to him on a silver platter. Her flesh was soft and yielding when he carefully entered her. This was not like having sex with a Mexican *puta*. He was shaking inside as he sought her easy like. She began to respond to him and soon became really excited. After their session, they both collapsed.

"You all right, Jane?"

She moaned, "No, you have made me more lost."

He rose up on his arms. "You all right?"

She pulled him down smiling. "I'm teasing you."

"Teasing?"

"Burl, I love you. I'm teasing you. You're wonderful. I don't think I have done this before, but I love it and you. Please take me to the clouds again."

"Damn right, girl. We're going to make you a helluva wife, hang on."

From there on, they were lost in a wild ride that ended with them in a pile and they slept.

He never what knew a wife would be like. He soon found out.

Every night she greeted him in their bed like a fresh wave. He had heard about wives who had headaches. Jane never had one—never denied him her body, never acted less than thrilled at their loving, and he felt spoiled beyond most men, rich or poor. He built her a *hacienda* and before long, they had two children. His ranching operation spread out, and in five years' time, he became one of the more prosperous cattlemen in southeast Arizona Territory.

One afternoon, three men rode up the drive on horseback. Skirt in hand, Jane hurried from the porch to see what they wanted. She paused at the iron-gate under the arch before she opened it. The unshaven men in their dust floured clothing were not who she had expected. Tough men with the hard eyes of wolves looked upon her like hungry *lobos*.

Her heart stopped in her chest. Why did the one in the center look so familiar?

"Gawdammit, Claire, ain't you going to come out and hug me, darling?" The man got off his horse and about caught his boot in the stirrup. The horse shied from him. He beat it about the face with the reins and cursed. He still fought with the panicked horse and at last gave up and tossed the reins to another. "Ain't you glad to see me Claire? I just got out of prison, baby. Don't that mean nothin' to you?"

"I don't even know who you are, mister."

"You remember when I broke out of that jail in Thatcher and we came down here on our way to Mexico?" He stuck a cigar in his mouth. "I guess we were real drunk that day. You were sleeping in the back of the wagon when the horses ran off."

"I—I don't know...."

"Well, darling, the law got us before we got to the border and I never could figure out where I lost you out of that damn wagon. A con told me in prison you might be right here. He said you lost your memory after falling out of a wagon. Damned if you ain't pretty as ever."

"Stay right there. I don't know you. I don't *want* to know you. Get on your horses and ride from here."

"Aw, Claire—I been in Yuma prison five years. You're still my wife and, baby, I need you bad today." His hand dropped below his belt and he massaged his crotch with lewd, exaggerated gestures.

"Mister, you better mount up and ride out of here." She closed her eyes. She'd never been his wife, and she sure didn't know him.

"Cover me, boys—"

Burl arrived, stepped in the archway and gently moved her over. "Let me handle them."

"I don't know them. I swear."

"Who in the hell are you?" The felon went for his gun. His years in prison must have slowed his draw, because the Colt in Burl's hand struck him twice in the chest. From behind him, two rifles barked, sounding as one, as his boys joined the fray. The pair of other *hombre*s pitched off their horses into the dust of the yard.

Jane sat on the ground sobbing. Burl holstered his gun and told the boys to go see about them. Kneeling, he raised her wet face and kissed her softly on the lips.

"I heard him, Jane. Your bad dream is finally over" Another gunshot cut off his words. Micah had just finished one of the outlaws off. "Jane, come get up. This nightmare is finally over. We heard what happened."

He pulled her to her feet.

"He was familiar, but I still don't recall him." They squeezed each other.

"Who in the hell wanted to remember him?"

She smiled at him like she did on their wedding day back in Tombstone. "Thank goodness for you and those boys being here today. I don't know what would have happened if you weren't. I'm so happy it's all over. You were the gift of a loving God that day you found me, and I've never been so thankful for you as I am today."

Burl pulled her tight. "You're not the only one He gave a gift to that day."

# DUSTY RICHARDS

Dusty Richards grew up riding horses and watching his western heroes on the big screen. He even wrote book reports for his classmates, making up westerns since English teachers didn't read that kind of book. But his mother didn't want him to be a cowboy, so he went to college, then worked for Tyson Foods, announced rodeos, and auctioned cattle across the country when he wasn't working as a radio announcer or television morning news anchor.

But his lifelong dream was to write the novels he loved. He sat on the stoop of Zane Grey's cabin and promised that he'd get published. In 1992, his first book, *Noble's Way*, hit the shelves. Dusty had another long-held dream, however—creating a publication dedicated to returning the West in all its glory—good and bad—back to the forefront of the modern American mindset. In 2014, he co-founded *Saddlebag Dispatches*, a magazine committed to doing just what he'd hoped. The proof of that dream you now hold in your hands.

# CATTLE COUPLETS AND EQUINE QUATRAINS

*The National Cowboy Poetry Gathering celebrates cowboy life from different cultures around the world.*

### Rod Miller

Interstate Highway I-80 follows the lazy Humboldt River Across northern Nevada along a trail blazed in days past by hundreds of thousands of California-bound 49ers and settlers and, later, the transcontinental railroad. At about milepost 300, I-80 slices through Elko. The city (voted America's Best Small City in 1990) was born as a way station for the railroad and survived as a supply base for scores of sprawling cattle ranches. Today, it fills that same job for America's most productive gold mines as well.

On a normal day, Elko's population hovers around 20,000. But every winter, starting the last week of January, the population swells by some 10,000 as cowboys and Western enthusiasts from around the West and the nation—around the world, really—come to town for the National Cowboy Poetry Gathering.

Cooked up in 1985 by folklorists from Western states, the Gathering brought together cowboys who recited poetry from days gone by about Western life,

as well as poets who penned their own creations about cowboy work and ways. The Western Folklife Center, headquartered in Elko's historic Pioneer Hotel building, organizes the event. Over the years, the Gathering grew to include cowboy and Western musicians, workshops on arts and crafts related to cowboy life, educational exhibits, and other cultural activities.

Setting its sights beyond the American West, the Gathering imports poets and purveyors of folk arts born of livestock traditions around the world. Representatives from Australia and Canada are on hand most every year. Herders from Argentina, Brazil, Mexico, France, Great Britain, Mongolia, and elsewhere have been featured. The 2018 Gathering honored Basques from the Pyrenees as well as descendants of Basques who immigrated in years past to work on American ranches.

POPULAR DAKOTA POETS **RODNEY NELSON** (NORTH) AND **YVONNE HOLLENBECK** (SOUTH) ON THE MAIN STAGE AT THE NATIONAL COWBOY POETRY GATHERING.

THE **ELKO CONVENTION CENTER** IS GROUND ZERO FOR THE **NATIONAL COWBOY POETRY GATHERING** EVERY JANUARY.

But, mostly, it's all about cowboy poetry, spiced with music. Poets and musicians take to stages in several rooms at the Elko Convention Center and adjacent Conference Center, and the Western Folklife Center downtown, to recite and read and sing all day long. And with evening shows at the Folklife Center's G Three Bar Theater and the 1,000-seat Convention Center auditorium, the momentum carries on well into the night. Other events and activities around Elko, both related to and independent of the official Gathering, include gear shows, art exhibits, jam sessions, lectures, food events, and on and on and on.

And to think it all started more than three decades ago with a handful of cowboy poets and a few hundred curious onlookers. But word spread and people came to Elko—no easy task, given its relative isolation on northern Nevada's high desert—and they keep coming. The Western Folklife Center estimates around 7,000 fans attended paid events this year. Thousands more come to town to be part of it all.

Where do they come from? "Everywhere" would not be an overstatement. Alis Gilleran came from Dallas,

Texas. And she didn't come alone. Her grandfather—Hardy Lee Seay, Jr., "Paw Paw," a lifetime rancher and musician—turned 80 in January. "So, this year, for his birthday, me and my mother and my aunt and my uncle and his wife and my aunt's husband all pitched in to pay for him to come up here and get to do this," Alis says.

"We love seeing people enjoy the same stuff we do, and introduce us to new stuff," Alis says of the music and poetry. "What I've particularly enjoyed and what I imagine Paw Paw has really enjoyed, is getting to hear people of varying ages talk about the rancher lifestyle. He works cattle for a living every day. It's been his whole life. And we think it's important to keep that going, and all the things that come with that lifestyle."

It is the family's first visit to the Gathering and Alis's introduction to a whole new world. "I'm going to be honest. I've never been to a poetry reading until yesterday. I could not have enjoyed it more—it was so great. I was just blown away by how much I enjoyed it. And I heard Paw Paw laughing a lot, so I think he enjoyed it too. I'm actually impressed by how much there is going on. I really didn't know what to expect. I knew that there were workshops and shows and things, but this is a big deal." The family hopes their first visit won't be the last, and Alis intends to again make the nearly 1,500-mile trip to Elko.

Brian Crane's trip to the Gathering from Sparks, Nevada, though not nearly so long, was also his first. "I've lived in Nevada for 30 or 40 years and have been hearing about the Poetry Gathering for years and never have gone. So I thought, well, I was looking for a road trip and this looked like a good one."

Author and artist of the popular newspaper comic strip "Pickles," Brian's character Earl Pickles has tried cowboy poetry in a few cartoon series. "He has dabbled his toe into the murky waters of cowboy poetry a time or two, but he's strictly an amateur," Brian says. "I got a lot of good response from readers, a lot of positive feedback, so I thought maybe this trip here would inspire a few more."

Far from a first-timer, "Sam" Beam has been coming to Elko for the Gathering since 1988. "I love everything about it," she says. "The music, the poetry, the gear, the people. My daughter, for the first time, came down

ALIS GILLERAN

BRIAN CRANE

"SAM" BEAM

AN ESTIMATED **7,000 PEOPLE** ATTENDED PAID SHOWS; THOUSANDS MORE ATTEND OTHER EVENTS.

AMY HALE AUCKER

DW GROETHE

when she was 17. We asked her what she wanted for Christmas, she said 'I want to go to Elko.' And she came down many years in a row."

Like many who attend the Gathering, Sam says there's a family feel to the event. "You come down every year and you meet new people. I'm still in touch with people I met 30 years ago that come from different states. I've met people from all over the world here."

Many cowboy poetry fans from around the world became fans thanks to the CowboyPoetry.com website. For nearly two decades, Margo Metegrano has ramrodded the site, which includes thousands of poems, feature stories on poets and poetry, history, how-to essays—well, if it's related to cowboy poetry, you'll find it on CowboyPoetry.com.

Margo has been a fixture at the National Cowboy Poetry Gathering since 2002, traveling lately from across the continent from Bar-D Ranch headquarters at Lexington, Virginia. "It definitely nourishes your soul to be in Elko and to see friends who become like family—and for the poetry and the music," she says.

## FROM THE OTHER SIDE OF THE MICROPHONE

There would not be a cowboy poetry gathering without cowboy poets. There's a ready supply of reciters and writers from all over the country, and they stand in line to be invited to perform in Elko. The Western Folklife Center receives hundreds of applications from poets and musicians every year and uses a rigorous selection process to choose the 50 or so who will be invited.

Bainville, Montana, poet, singer, and songwriter DW Groethe has been featured as both a poet and musician many times over the years. He has also served on the selection committee. "The way you get picked is about as fair as it's going to get," DW says. "There are three people, and they get to pick. Somebody represents poets, somebody represents music, and there's somebody from the folklorist world. And it's those three who listen and pick. I think if you're picked once, you should be honored."

The process seems to work, as the quality of talent at Elko is as good as it gets. "Most of the folks that are invited here are damn good at what they do and they are the best," DW says. "It's a right joy to be included among them. And it's probably one of the finest ways, if you're listening, to learn how to improve your own work."

Jerry "Brooksie" Brooks is a long-time reciter at Elko, as well as other cowboy poetry events around the country. What makes Elko different? "Elko's Elko—the granddaddy of them all. And that's all there is to it. It's not a describable thing. Let Elko happen to you," she says. "If I'm performing, I try to remember to ask how many are here for the first time, and I envy them so much because I remember that moment, that epiphany, when the Elko 'wash' just inundated me. It's an 'experienceable' thing, but not really that describable."

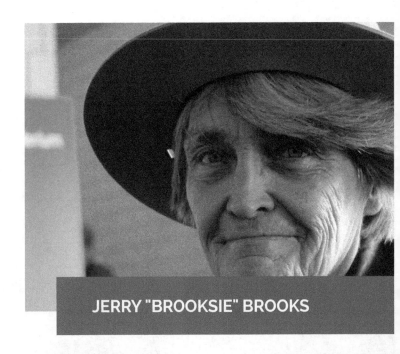

JERRY "BROOKSIE" BROOKS

Newer to Elko stages is Jarle Kvale. Nowadays, he's the program director at a small public radio station on the Turtle Mountain Chippewa Indian Reservation in north-central North Dakota. "I'm a cowboy poet and I've always enjoyed cowboy poetry and Western music," Jarle says. "I've been doing open mics here for the last four or five years, and last year I got to be an invited performer here." Jarle also had the opportunity to fill in for an absent poet at the 2018 Gathering.

Among the criteria the selection committee considers is authenticity. Invited performers must have legitimate cowboy credentials, whether it's background or experience in ranching, rodeo, livestock raising, cowboy work, or other aspects of rural Western life. Jarle says that's important. "I think the worst thing is to be a fake. I think people can see through that. The crowds here, they're really into every word that's being said."

JARLE KVALE

Terry Nash, a Loma, Colorado, cowboy, made his second appearance this year as an invited performer. He believes the rigor of the selection process contributes to the quality of the event. "There's an anonymous committee that looks over your application, looks at your background. They want to know you have a ranch or cowboy background. I applied a lot of times before I finally got an invitation," Terry says. "I was jazzed. I was just tickled. I couldn't quit grinning. It was really redeeming to me when I got that second invitation because I figured I must have done something right the first time. I go to a lot of gatherings, but it's a special thing when you get this invitation."

TERRY NASH

POETS, RECITERS, SONGWRITERS, SINGERS, AND SCHOLARS **ANDY WILKINSON** AND **ANDY HEDGES** CAME TO THE GATHERING FROM LUBBOCK, TEXAS.

## AND NOW A WORD FROM THE SPONSOR

Putting together the National Cowboy Poetry Gathering is a year-round job at the Western Folklife Center. It's not all they do—they curate exhibits, produce radio features and television documentaries, and do fieldwork and research around the West, focusing on rural culture. But the Cowboy Poetry Gathering is the big show. The word "National" was added to the name when the United States Senate passed a resolution in 2000 designating it as such. The renovated Pioneer Hotel in downtown Elko is home to the Center's offices and its Wiegand Gallery, 300-seat G Three Bar Theater, 20-seat black box theater, gift shop, and historic saloon.

A long list of sponsors and donors provides much of the funding, along with Western Folklife Center stakeholders and members from across the country and the world. And given its relatively small and over-extended staff, the Western Folklife Center relies on legions of volunteers to pull off logistics at the annual Gathering. Among them are shuttle drivers, ticket sellers and takers, program hosts, gift shop personnel, bartenders, food servers, door monitors, and docents.

And security guards.

THE BIG SHOWS ARE HELD IN THE **CONVENTION CENTER AUDITORIUM** BEFORE AUDIENCES OF A THOUSAND APPRECIATIVE FANS.

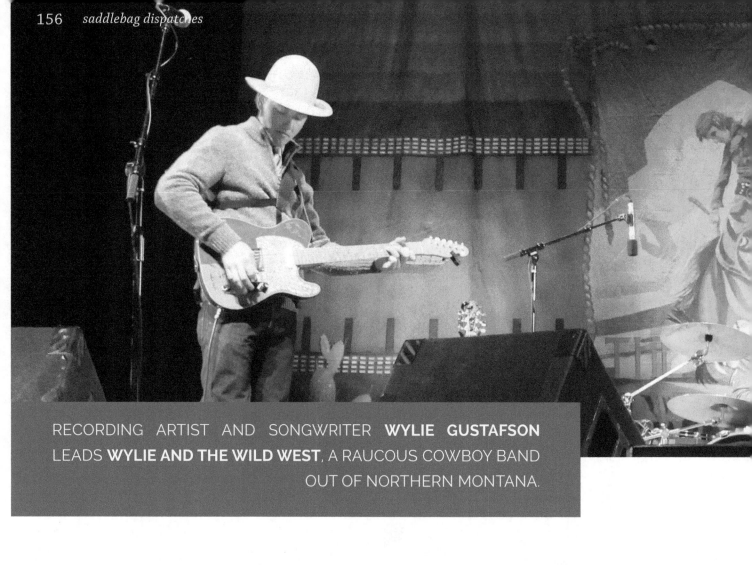

RECORDING ARTIST AND SONGWRITER **WYLIE GUSTAFSON** LEADS **WYLIE AND THE WILD WEST**, A RAUCOUS COWBOY BAND OUT OF NORTHERN MONTANA.

No one knows that end of the event better than Elko resident Milt Grisham, who volunteered at the first Gathering in 1985 and at every one since. "I've been here, every one of them," he says. He believes the event benefits the community. "It is good for Elko, absolutely. It's a big gathering point, and it's a point of interest for everyone. You get people from all over the world show up. It's been good for Elko."

Milt doesn't know if he'll be back for the 2019 Gathering. "I hit 93 last July. I've been doing this a long time, so I'm getting a little tired. This might be the last year because I've been doing it forever and ten days."

But, if Milt feels able, it's a good bet you'll see him at the next National Cowboy Poetry Gathering. As hundreds and hundreds of poets and musicians, and thousands and thousands of fans know, it's hard to stay away. As reciter Jerry Brooks says, "What else would I be doing? If this is here, where else would I be?"

**MILT GRISHAM**

*—Spur Award-winning writer Rod Miller is the author of* Goodnight Goes Riding and Other Poems, Things a Cowboy Sees and Other Poems, *as well as several works of fiction and history about the West. His latest novel is* Rawhide Robinson Rides a Dromedary, *with* Father unto Many Sons *due out in the fall. Find him online at* **www. writerRodMiller.com.**

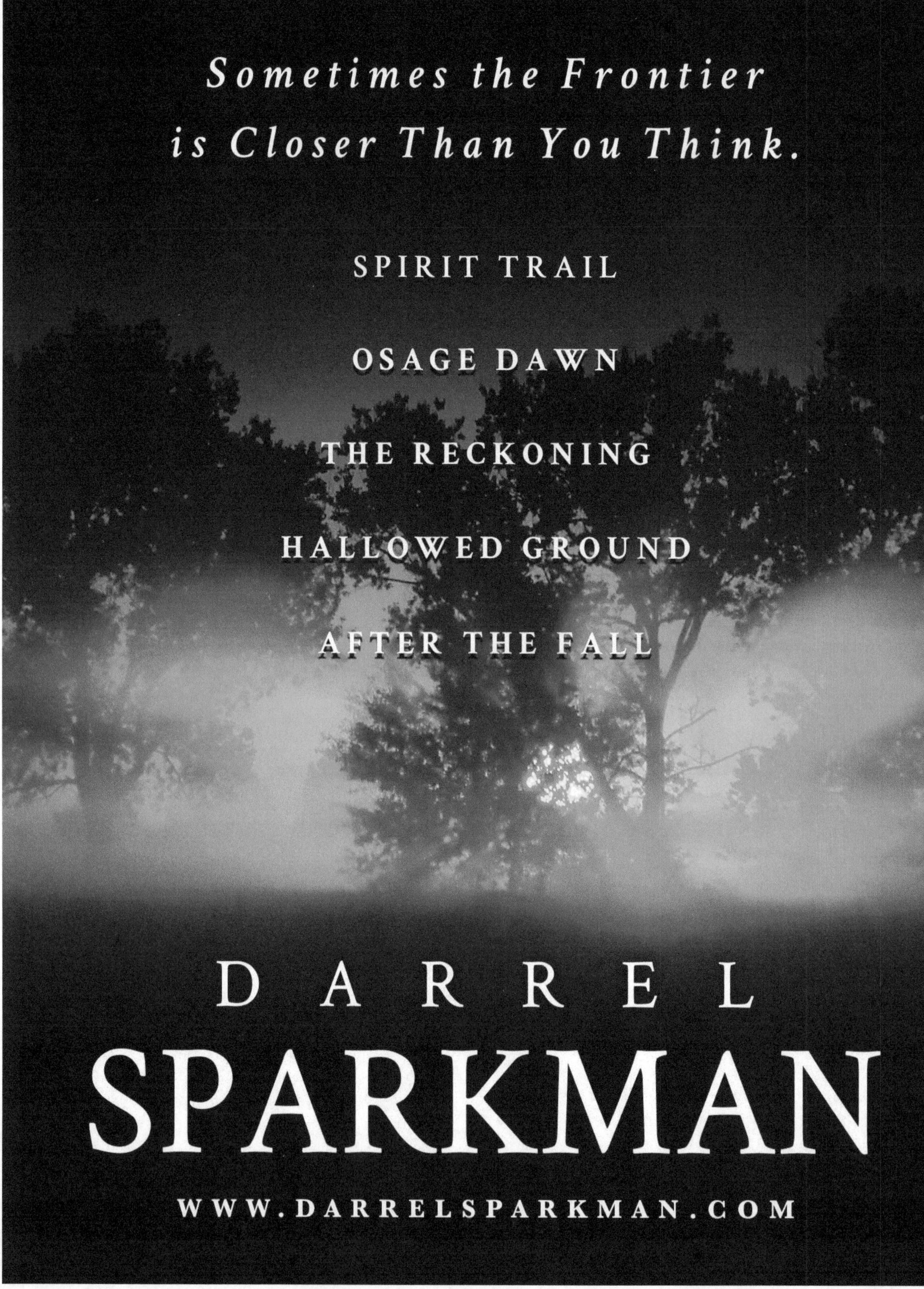
Sometimes the Frontier
is Closer Than You Think.
SPIRIT TRAIL
OSAGE DAWN
THE RECKONING
HALLOWED GROUND
AFTER THE FALL
DARREL
SPARKMAN
WWW.DARRELSPARKMAN.COM

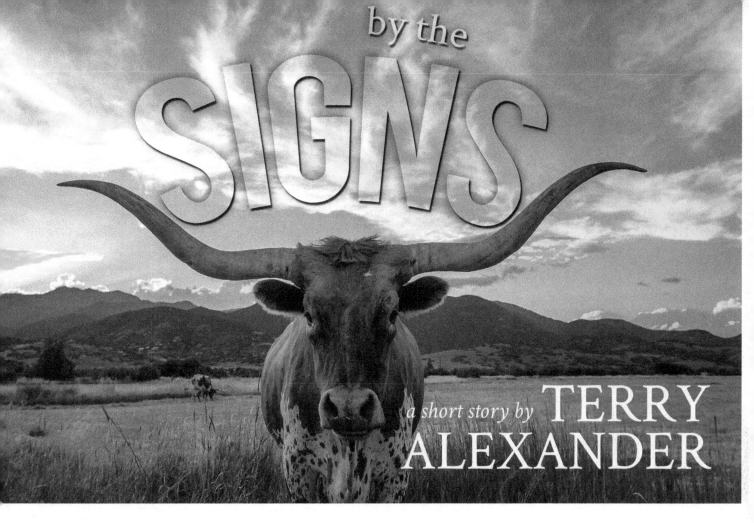

# by the
# SIGNS

*a short story by* TERRY ALEXANDER

Mr. Tillman." An old man, tall and reed thin, swung his leg over the saddle and stepped down from his black horse. He yanked his hat from his head and rolled it in his hands. "I don't want to tell you your business, but we shouldn't castrate them young bull calves right now. The signs is all wrong."

"I don't want to hear it, Royce." A heavy man shook his head. He held the reins of the chestnut stud in a tight grip. The expensive saddle under him creaked as he moved. "I want those animals taken care of today."

"Mr. Tillman, we cut them calves today, half of them will bleed to death before we can get it stopped. The signs are right in the belly, sure sign those animals won't do well. If we wait a week to ten days the signs are a lot better. They're down in the ankles, the animals won't have a lick of trouble then."

"Dale, you're foreman." Tillman looked at the man on the piebald gelding. "What do you think, is there anything to Royce and this sign nonsense?"

Dale scratched at the lump on his nose, from where it had been broken years ago. "Lot of folks set great store by what the signs are, mostly farmers. They like to plant crops when the signs are right. They think it leads to a better harvest."

"What about cattlemen? What do they think about following the signs?"

"Mr. Tillman, me and my brothers can have them bulls rounded up and put the blade to them in three hours, easy." A big man with a block jaw kneed his small paint into the circle. "We can make steers out of the entire bunch of them double quick, just give us the word." He cast a hard look at Royce and Dale.

"Mr. Tillman, a lot of the ranchers around here go by the signs." Dale said.

Tillman stared at his foreman. "Do you like your job here, Dale?"

"Yes, sir, I do. Best job I've ever had."

"Then you need to do what you're told." Tillman pulled a sack of tobacco and some rolling papers from his vest. He slowly rolled a smoke, keeping his eyes on Dale while he completed the task. "I pay good money for the best ranch hands. I expect my orders to be carried out double quick." He scratched a match to life on his saddle horn and held it under the cigarette. "Now, I want those young bulls castrated today. Do you understand?" A wreath of smoke surrounded his head.

"Mr. Tillman." Royce reached over and grabbed the black's reins. "If you're set on working them calves today, let's drive them over to Bright's Corral and take our time doing this. We don't want those animals running everywhere and get their blood to pumping fast beforehand. If we can do this without stressing them too bad, they might be okay."

"You worry too much, old man." The big man shook his head. "Them calves'll be fine. They'll be sore for two or three days after we finish, but they'll heal alright."

"Calvin, you don't know squat about cattle." Royce turned and stared up at the big man on the pinto. "You're just a hard-headed fool who can't think beyond the end of his nose."

Calvin squeezed his saddle horn. A red flush crept up his face. "Just because yore an old man, don't mean I won't whup you like a wormy dog."

"They'll be none of that," Tillman shouted. "Ain't gonna be no fighting on my range." His hard eyes fastened on Royce. "If you ain't willing to do what I tell you, when I tell you to do it, then you need to get off my place, Royce."

Royce licked his lips. "It's not that I don't want to do things yore way, Mr. Tillman, it's just that there's a better way, a smarter way to do things."

"He just said you wuz stupid, Mr. Tillman." Calvin laughed. "Guess he thinks he's the smartest man around these parts."

"That ain't what I meant." Royce glared at the big man. "Mr. Tillman, if you get those calves hot and then castrate them today, some of them are gonna bleed out. I'm telling you the signs are all wrong."

"How many days work do I owe you for?" Tillman scratched his whiskered jaw.

"You owe me for eight days work." Royce glanced down toward his boots.

Tillman patted his vest pockets. "Here's a gold

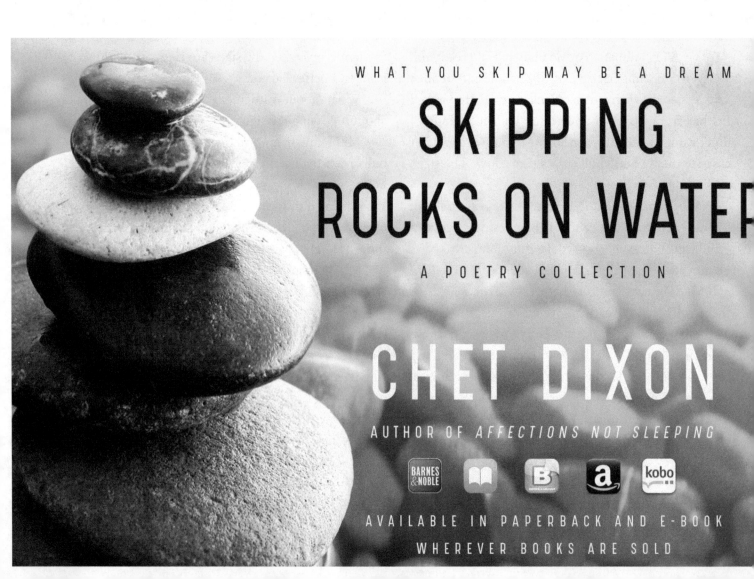

eagle. Get back to the bunk house and get your gear and get off my land."

"Yes, sir." Royce jammed his hat on his head and slipped his foot in the stirrup, swinging up into the saddle. He turned to Dale. "Don't let them fools run those calves before they castrate them. Some of them will die for sure if you do."

The foreman nodded. "Hate to see you go, Royce."

"Keep talking like that, and you can go with him." Tillman said.

"I'll do what you tell me, Mr. Tillman." Dale nodded.

Royce held the reins lightly in his hand. He turned the black gelding and touched his spurs to the animal's side. The horse moved forward slowly.

"Boys, I want those calves castrated today. Now run those animals down while I get the coal oil ready." Tillman's voice reached his ears. Royce spurred his gelding into a gallop.

—

**Royce sat near the** small campfire. He moved the coffee pot from the fire and sat it on the flat rock allowing the grounds to settle. He gazed over to the black horse. He'd staked it out on a long rope earlier to allow it to graze in a wide circle. "Never figured on coming back to this place. Figured I'd let Mr. Tillman use it for graze from now on," he mumbled to himself.

He took a worn out glove and grabbed the handle of the coffeepot and filled the tin cup beside the fire. Royce lifted the cup to his mouth and blew across the surface of the coffee. The horse stamped its feet and gazed off into the darkness. He placed the cup on one of the rocks surrounding the fire and moved his rifle closer to hand

"Royce, that you over there?" a voice called.

"Yeah, Dale. It's me." He propped the rifle against the saddle. "Come on in, I've got coffee on."

Dale eased the piebald near the fire. "You know me, I never turned down a cup of coffee. Let me take care of this knothead, and I'll be right there." He swung his leg over the saddle and stepped to the ground. He hung the near stirrup on the saddle horn and loosened the girth, easing the saddle to the ground. After he

removed the blanket, he took a handful of grass and wiped the animal down.

"Be alright if I stake him out there close to yours?" he asked

"Shore, go ahead." Royce nodded. "I've got an extra stake peg, if you need one."

"Naw, I've got one." He removed his rope from the saddle and pulled a metal stake from his saddle bag and marched out into the darkness. He returned within a few minutes, carrying the bridle. "That coffee smells good."

"Drag yore cup out and get a cup." Royce stared at his former supervisor over the rim of the tin cup. "Why are you here, Dale?"

"You were right about those bulls. Calvin and his brothers ran those animals for over twenty minutes, just for the fun of it. They got them down by Bright's Corral, and set to work." Dale sat cross-legged in front of his saddle. "You were right about Calvin and Max. Those two are plum loco, now Phil, he'll make a good cowman one day. He'll listen to people."

"How many died?" Royce blew on his coffee and sipped at the surface.

"Three died outright. Soon as they cut them animals, Calvin swatted them with his rope and got them to running all over again." Dale glanced at the older man. "He didn't put more than a dab of coal oil on them bulls either."

"Tillman'll be lucky, if he don't lose the whole bunch."

"Tillman fired Calvin and Max after the third steer dropped to the ground. Phil wouldn't stay on without his brothers and he quit. Mr. Tillman paid them off and they rode back to the ranch to get their gear." Dale paused to sip at his coffee. "They rode in to Lee Springs. Figure they'll spend all their money at the saloon. Then, well, you know…"

"You figure they'll get to thinking about me? Maybe blame me cause they got fired?" Royce drained his cup and slung the dregs into the fire. "You planning on babysitting me?"

"Nope, just gonna make sure it stays between you and Calvin." Dale sipped at his coffee. "Mr. Tillman wants to talk to you about buying your land here."

"You know I ain't gonna do that. I ain't got a lot of land, but by God it belongs to me and I'm gonna hang onto it for as long as I can. Time comes I want to be buried here." Royce drained the cup and placed it on the rock next to the fire. "Think I'll get some shut eye. If yore right, I figure them three should ride in about daylight."

"I'm gonna finish this cup. Then I'll grab some sleep myself. I'll make sure we're up before daylight."

"Dale, you ain't ever woke up any morning before me. Doubt you'll do it tomorrow." Royce pulled his blanket up to his shoulders and laid his head back on his saddle. "Hope you sleep peaceable." He closed his eyes. Within seconds the old man was snoring.

—

**Royce glanced at his** sleeping companion when Dale rolled over and opened his left eye. "'Bout time you woke up. It must be nearly six."

"That coffee smells good. Hope it's better than that hog wash you brewed last night." He tossed back his blanket. "Are those eggs?" He glanced down at a small frying pan.

"Sho nuff. I found a nest of bird eggs back in the trees, got lucky only one had a bird inside. Figured they'd taste pretty good this morning. I know it ain't much, but it should get us through the morning." He filled a tin cup with coffee and passed it to Dale. "I heard Calvin and his brothers about an hour ago. They was following our trail and lost it. They took the left fork up at the big oak. They must still be half drunk."

"They'll figger out their mistake soon. Soon as we wolf down these eggs we can start back to the ranch." Dale blew across the surface of the tin cup and sipped the dark brew.

"I ain't going back to the ranch. Remember Mr. Tillman paid me off." Royce forked two of the eggs

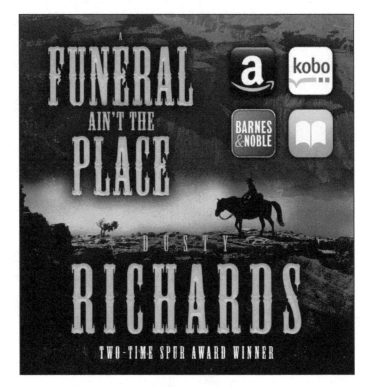

into a tin plate and passed it to Dale. "I've got a few cows and calves on this place. Figure I'll work my own stock fer awhile."

"You're going to stay out here and work ten or twelve cows by yourself?" Dale said. "Hell, you ain't even got a shanty out here."

"I can build one. I got some nice sized trees down by the crick, and my hands can fit a chopping ax." Royce took a sip of coffee and placed the tin cup on the circle of stones surrounding the fire. "Sounds like our company has finally arrived."

"Let me handle things." Dale placed his plate near the fire and grabbed for his pistol.

"Sit down, this is my place." Royce stood near the fire, his fisted hands resting on his hips. He watched as the three brothers came through the trees and rode to his campsite. "Nice to see you boys, why don't you lite down and drink some coffee."

"I come here to settle your hash, Old Man." Calvin swayed in the saddle. He passed his reins over to Max and swung his leg over the saddle. He lost his grip on the saddle horn and tumbled to the ground, his left foot caught in the stirrup. The horse turned and looked at the man sprawled under his feet.

"That's a well-trained animal, lest it would have kicked you square in the head." Royce grabbed Calvin's worn out boot and worked it free of the stirrup. "Ready fer that coffee."

Calvin rolled to his belly and pushed himself to his knees. "I'm gonna whup you. All yore talking got us fired off a good job."

"I don't figger you can whup anybody from thar," Royce snickered.

"You just give me a second to get to my legs under

me." Calvin fought his way to his feet, and staggered toward Royce.

Royce moved away from Calvin's wide, swinging blow. The big man couldn't regain his balance and fell to the ground. "You sure you don't want that coffee?" he asked.

"Damn it, I don't want no coffee. I just want you to stay still and fight me fair." Calvin rolled to his feet and placed his hand in the fire. "Great God All Mighty." He screamed. He yanked his hand from the embers and knocked the tin cup of coffee free and onto his chest. The hot liquid soaked into his shirt and burned his chest. ""Oh Lord. Oh Lord," he yelled.

"Let me get him," Max shouted. "I ain't as drunk as you are."

"Leave him alone, Max." Phil grabbed his brother's arm. "Royce didn't do anything to us. Calvin's the one that got us fired. He always thinks he's so smart, that he knows everything. Look at him laying down there. Royce could be stomping his brains in right now if he wanted to. You two spent all the money we had on whiskey last night. We ain't got nothing left and we don't even have a job."

"I don't think Calvin hurt his hand very bad, couple days rest and it should be good as new." Royce said. "Sure you boys don't want some coffee."

"This old jasper makes some pretty good brew." Dale nodded. "I might have something in my saddle bags that would help that burn."

Calvin rolled to a sitting position, holding his head with both hands. "First time I was ever whipped and not even hit." He turned and looked at his brothers. "I'm gonna find a doctor. You two help me get in the saddle."

"I'll do it." Royce said. "Doubt Max could find the ground." He caught the big man under the arms and helped him to his feet. The older man walked by his side to the gelding. "Dale, help me get this galoot into the saddle." They placed his boot in the stirrup and boosted him into the leather.

Phil nodded as he watched his brothers turn to ride away. "Is that coffee as good as Dale said?"

"Climb on down and have a cup." Royce grinned.

# TERRY ALEXANDER

Terry Alexander and his wife Phyllis live on a small farm near Porum, Oklahoma. They have three children, 13 grandchildren and one great granddaughter. Terry is a member of The Oklahoma Writers Federation, Ozark Creative Writers, Tahlequah Writers, Storytellers of America (Ozarks Original Chapter), Western Writers of America and the Western Fictioneers. If you see him at a conference, though, don't let him convince you to take part in one of his trivia games—he'll stump you every time.

*By the Signs* is Terry's third short story to appear in *Saddlebag Dispatches*. He has also been published in various anthologies from Airship 27, Pro Se Press, Pulp Modern, Big Pulp, and several others, and has won multiple awards for his work. He also writes a quarterly column entitled "Let's Talk Westerns" where he shares his voluminous knowledge of classic Western pop culture, entertainment, and esoteric trivia nobody else could possibly know... and it's likely he made up.

# BLUE *diamond*

## *a poem*

Ode to you ranch woman, rare as the blue diamond

coyote clean and spiritually unassailable

procreated to make hay, feed stock and ride

miles of tough grass, saddle-sore and sick calves

you double rope, head on, worry-weathered

flank your partner on the prairie, in the barn, at the bank

knowing the wise side of a hard dollar, what to do

with a profit and when there is not, your persistence

breaks trail and after-hours are nothing new

with a casserole in the oven and a baby at your breast, you mend

worn denim, old socks, the unsung melody of no regret

And only

when all things are fed and safe in place, do you crawl into bed

your wind-burnt skin laced with lavender, warm flannelette

a silhouette of salt and prayer, you sleep on the short side of another tomorrow

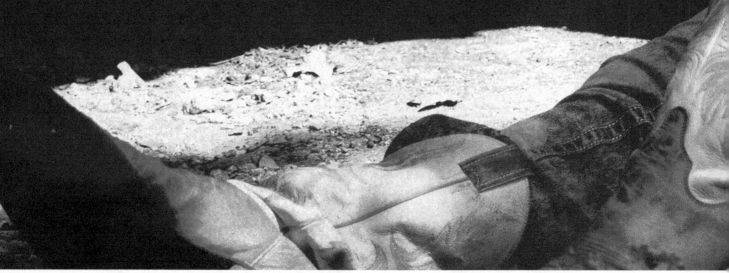

SADDLEBAG

POETRY

laurie

muirhead

# *shortgrass*
# COUNTRY

**John J. Dwyer**

*historical columnist*

The larger-than-life biography of the good and great Charles Colcord (1859-1934) reads like a half-century chronicle of territorial and early statehood Oklahoma and the old Southwest, or at least of its most dramatic events. Born before the Civil War and living nearly until World War II, this iron-willed Westerner and consummate man of action helped blaze the Chisholm Trail, partnered in building one of the greatest cattle dynasties of nineteenth-century America, and rode in three Oklahoma land runs.

He proved himself one of the greatest lawmen of the Old West and was the first police chief of Oklahoma City, the first sheriff of Oklahoma County, and a frontier U.S. Marshal. He built many of Oklahoma's first generation businesses, as well as its first skyscraper, the Colcord Building, which still thrives over a century later.

Twelve-year-old Charley Colcord's father William, a Confederate Civil War colonel from Kentucky, moved the boy from the New Orleans area to Texas to preserve his malaria-stricken life. The move proved a good one, as Charley was driving cattle up the Chisholm by the time he was fourteen. The daring, headstrong youth ran away from home at one point to cowboy on his own, then returned to tell his father about the need for horses in Kansas and the grazing lands open for rental from the Cherokees in the Cherokee Outlet.

## CATTLE KINGDOM

The elder Colcord moved his operation north and formed the Jug Cattle Company in northern Indian Territory and southern Kansas, with teenaged Charley the range boss. For a while, the Colcords lived in an earthen dugout. Then, from the late-1870s through the mid-1880s, William, Charley, and some of their neighbors proceeded to build one of the greatest cattle kingdoms in history, the Comanche Pool.

**CHARLES "CHUCK" COLCORD**

THE GOLD RUSH OF 1948

# GOLDEN WEST

JULY 1973
58450-1 PDC 50¢

PERSONAL
RECOLLECTIONS
OF CHIEF WASHAKIE

CHUCK
COLCORD:
SCOURGE OF
THE CATTLE
RUSTLERS

THE SECRET

THE **VERACITY** OF THE PARTICULAR **EXPLOITS** PORTRAYED IN THIS MAGAZINE IS **UNCERTAIN**, BUT THAT OF LAWMAN **CHARLES "CHUCK" COLCORD**'S **DEEDS INSPIRING THEM IS NOT.**

TAUGHT ABE LINCOLN

COLCORD WAS **OKLAHOMA CITY'S FIRST POLICE CHIEF, ITS FIRST SHERIFF, AND A DEPUTY U. S. MARSHAL IN OKLAHOMA TERRITORY**. HERE, IN AUGUST 1890, HE SITS WITH THE OTHER OFFICERS OF OKC'S FIRST POLICE DEPARTMENT. *COURTESY EDNA M. COUCH COLLECTION, OKLAHOMA HISTORICAL SOCIETY.*

They did so largely on reservation and other lands they leased from the Natives, which channeled enormous amounts of American dollars into tribal coffers. The Colcords battled brutal weather, including colossal open range blizzards, harsh terrain, wild animals, and periodically violent Indians. They cooperated with their colleagues in the Comanche Pool for the common defense and shared resources.

At its peak in the mid-1880s, the Pool ran more than eighty thousand cattle. Roundup time covered over three million acres that stretched across central and western Kansas, the length of western Indian Territory south to Red River, and west across Texas to its border with New Mexico. The cattlemen served customers as varied as New York City restaurants and the western Indian Territory reservations then hosting thousands of Natives. In 1885, the federal government broke up the Comanche Pool and others to hasten the way for American settlement of the Indian lands.

## WILD COWPUNCHER HUSBAND

The same year, Colcord married Harriet Scoresby, the daughter of an English-born Methodist Episcopal minister. As he recorded in his memorable The

Autobiography of Charles Francis Colcord, 1859-1934, he pursued his own path for this as with so many other things in his life:

*I went up to Elm Creek to attend a dance given by Mrs. Slack, an elder sister of Harriet Scoresby and fell violently in love with her at first sight and determined to have her for my wife. The second time I met Harriet I was driving a herd of cattle from the range into Kansas. Her father, her uncles and all other members of her family were bitterly opposed to Harriet marrying a wild cowpuncher. I made up my mind all the preachers in Kansas could not stop me. I talked to Harriet's brother-in-law, who lived in Barber County, Kansas and he told me the whole family was opposed to me because people had exaggerated reports about me. I think this brother-in-law did a lot towards breaking down this opposition and Harriet's mother, who was one of the greatest women I ever knew, was favorable toward me from the very start. Also a young brother, O. C. Storesby, who was something of a wild kid himself, seemed to take a liking to me and often helped me out in meeting his sister.*

Harriet and Charley wed on February 9, 1885, and remained so through flush and thin until his death a half-century later.

When disease decimated the already scattered cattle of the Comanche Pool and sunk the Colcord financial fortunes, Charley and Harriet migrated west to Arizona where he managed a ranch. His autobiography modestly recounts various adventures. These included sliding while mounted to the precipice of a mountain cliff, the horse partially protruding over it before Charley could bring them both out.

## PIONEER, LAWMAN, OIL BARON

The Colcords returned to present-day Oklahoma for the 1889 Unassigned Lands Run, which included present-day Oklahoma City, Norman, and the surrounding region. Still brimming with restless energy and daring as he entered his thirties, it was the first of three lands runs he rode in between 1889 and 1893. They netted him property in western, central, and northern Oklahoma.

He accepted a commission as U.S. Deputy Marshal in Perry and battled some of the most formidable outlaws in the Old West, including the Doolins and Daltons, and emerged with his life to tell about it. When Colcord's autobiography touches at all on such events, it does so with more modesty than others' accounts of his exploits. One notable scene he does recount is a shootout with a bullying saloon keeper wherein Colcord acted in self-defense, had the quicker draw, and wounded the man.

In 1898, the Colcords settled down in OKC. Now forty-two, thrifty, and hard-working, Charley rose quickly to leadership in the boisterous, fast-growing pioneer city. He founded one bank, served as vice president of another, president of the Oklahoma City Building & Loan Association, and director of the Oklahoma State Fair Association. He developed numerous residential areas and helped spearhead establishment of the first meat-packing firm in the Oklahoma City Stockyards, as well as the construction of both the Commerce Exchange Building and the swank Biltmore Hotel.

In 1901, Colcord, daredevil wildcatter Rob-

ert Galbreath, and others struck oil in the new Red Fork field, four miles west of the Arkansas River, across from the Creek-spawned village of Tulsa. Colcord shared his first-hand account of Oklahoma's first great oil boom:

> *In the spring of 1901 the Federal government sold at auction the town site of Red Fork, a new community on the Frisco line which was then building about three miles west of Tulsa. Robert Galbreath, representing Colcord, Galbreath and C. G. Jones, attended this sale and purchased twenty-five or thirty lots...Years later I heard stories of several fellows who drilled the first oil well in Red Fork, but for all these years I have felt that we were the first to strike oil there.*

Colcord, Galbreath, and Chesley suspected that much more oil lay south of Red Fork. Four years later, they were hunting in the area when Colcord's two Kentucky wolfhounds lit out after a wolf. While searching for the dogs, Chesley found oil seeping in plain daylight from surface rocks on land ten miles south of Tulsa owned by part-Creek Indian Ida Glenn and her family.

The Oklahomans secured a gaggle of leases from the Glenns in and around the area. They shrewdly plied their time until federal restrictions on drillers softened.

**COLCORD WITH BILL TILGHMAN**

Then they chose their spot, drilled nearly fifteen hundred feet down—a deep well for the era—and brought in the Ida Glenn Number One in late 1905. Numerous other wells followed for them. These comprised the famed Glenn Pool field, one of the mightiest on record.

COLCORD BUILT HIS **OKLAHOMA CITY MANSION** (PICTURED ABOVE) IN 1903, FOUR YEARS BEFORE OKLAHOMA STATEHOOD. IT WAS A REPLICA OF HIS FATHER'S PLANTATION HOME IN KENTUCKY AND **SYMBOLIZED THE ACCOMPLISHMENTS OF A PEOPLE WHO HAD RAISED UP A BOOMING AMERICAN CAPITAL CITY** FROM THE BARREN PRAIRIE IN JUST OVER A DECADE. *COURTESY OKLAHOMA HISTORICAL SOCIETY.*

It generated more revenue than the California Gold Rush and Colorado Silver Boom combined and helped build the new state of Oklahoma.

## FINAL ROARS

Oklahoma's roughhewn frontier ethos persisted well into the twentieth century, despite the building of skyscrapers—of which Colcord built its first—and major cities. The newly christened capital city of Oklahoma City hurtled to the brink of war in its streets during a 1911 streetcar strike. Out-of-state unions from up north and back east and their "muscle" encouraged streetcar workers disgruntled over wages and working conditions to strike.

Former Police Chief, Sheriff, and U.S. Marshal Colcord, taking command by experience, reputation, ability, and strength of character, stepped into the breach. He put out an alert from his downtown office that rippled across the city and its surrounding environs. It called for trustworthy men to drop whatever they were doing and head downtown, where he officed, and to come armed. Colcord marshaled hundreds of them from the city's business and middle and upper-class communities to confront the protestors. Colcord commanded more guns than his opponents and the steely will to use them. As often before and since that settled the issue peaceably.

In 1918, President Woodrow Wilson appointed

WHEN COMPLETED IN 1910, THE **COLCORD BUILDING** STOOD TWELVE STORIES TALL. IT WAS **OKLAHOMA CITY'S FIRST SKYSCRAPER** AND THE **TALLEST BUILDING IN THE STATE.**

him to the National Petroleum Conservation Board.

His civic and historic deeds did not prevent him from the greater deed of loving his one wife for the half-century until his death and siring and raising six children. He served as president of the Oklahoma Historical Society the last many years of his life and delivered a memorable speech in 1933, the year before his death. It constituted a virtual eyewitness account of the history of frontier Oklahoma.

The same year, at age seventy-four and only months away from the end of his life, Colcord rose up one final time as "Guardian" of Oklahoma. His close friend and fellow oilman Charles Urschel was kidnapped at gunpoint from his OKC residence by George "Machine Gun" Kelly, one of the most notorious gangsters in American history, and held for ransom. Colcord called Oklahoma City's wealthiest men to his Colcord Building and collected an enormous amount of money—not for a ransom payment, but for a reward on the head of Kelly. The vicious gangster was soon captured and Urschel returned unharmed.

Pearls of understanding and wisdom fill Colcord's autobiography. Not least are his crediting his career rise to having made good on previous commitments to men of leadership and means, who thus gained the confidence in him to participate with or back him in further ventures. Upon his 1934 gathering to his fathers, full of years and honor, the Oklahoma City Chamber of Commerce issued the following resolution:

*Affluence came to (Charles Colcord) but left unspoiled his native gentleness and simplicity. Always he was modest, humble, democratic, generous, just and kind. He remembered the less fortunate friends of his early days.*

Charley Colcord's Fairlawn Cemetery tombstone sits quietly amidst the city and state he labored so well to build into something special. It reads, appropriately:

*His life was gentle, and the elements*
*So mix'd in him, that Nature might stand up*

*—*

*And say to all the world, 'This was a man'*

—*John J. Dwyer is an author and regular contributor to* Saddlebag Dispatches. *In the past, he has worked as a History Chair at a classical college preparatory school, a newspaper publisher, and a radio host. He lives with Grace his wife of 28 years, their daughter Katie, and their grandson Luke.*

# let's talk

# WESTERNS

**Terry Alexander**

*western pop culture columnist*

Maria Cristina Estrella Marcela Jurado de Garcia was born on January sixteenth, 1924 in Guadalajara, Jalisco, Mexico. Known to western fans by the much shorter name of Katy Jurado. She began her career as a Mexican film, stage, and television actress in Mexico in 1943 in the film *No Maturas*. Her family was against her chosen profession. She married Victor Velazquez in 1943 at sixteen to escape her family's control. They had two children together, Victor Hugo and Sandra. They divorced in 1946. In 1951, Budd Boettcher and John Wayne saw her at a bullfight in Mexico, and Boettcher brought her to Hollywood for a small part in his film. *The Bullfighter and the Lady,* with Robert Stack, Gilbert Roland, Joy Page and Virginia Page. During the filming, Katy spoke her lines phonetically, since she didn't speak or understand English.

In 1952, director Stanley Cramer cast her as saloon owner Helen Ramirez in the classic western *High Noon.* The movie starred Gary Cooper, Grace Kelly, Lloyd Bridges, and Lon Chaney, Jr. Katy learned to speak English for the role. She took lessons for two hours a day for two months, before filming began. This film earned her a Golden Globe for best-supporting actress. The first Latin American actress to win this award.

Joseph Kane directed Katy in *San Antone* in 1953, she played Mistania Figueroa. The film starred Rod Cameron, Arleen Whelan, Forrest Tucker, Bob Steele, and Harry Carey, Jr. Carl Miller (Cameron), a Texas cowboy led a cattle drive into French-held Mexico to exchange the herd for fifty prisoners being held by former Confederate officer Brian Culver (Tucker), who once double-crossed him.

She also made *Arrowhead* that same year, directed by Charles Marquis Warren. The film starred Charlton Heston as Indian Scout Ed Bannon. It featured Jack Palance as Toriano the son of an Apache chief who was educated in the east and returned to lead his people. Brian Keith, Milburn Stone, Frank DeKova, and Robert J. Wilke also appeared in the film. Katy portrayed Nita, an evil Comanche woman and the love interest of Heston's character Bannon.

In 1954 she appeared in director Edward Dmytryk's *Broken Lance.* The film starred Spencer Tracy, Robert Wagner, Jean Peters, Richard Widmark, Hugh O'Brian, Earl Holliman, and E. G. Marshall. Katy played the *Senora*, an Indian woman married to Spencer Tracy and the mother of Robert Wagner. She was called the *Senora* to hide her Indian heritage. Katy was nominated for an Academy Award for her role, setting the bar again as she was the first Latin American actress to be nominated for an Oscar.

After a two year break, she returned to the western genre in 1956 with the movie, *Man from Del Rio* directed by Harry Horner and starring Anthony Quinn, Peter Whitney, and Whit Bissell. Katy played Estella, Quinn's love interest. Dave Robles (Quinn) a Mexican gunman came to the town of Mesa, he killed a few notorious gunmen, including the outlaw-turned-lawman of the town, who was working for a man that actually controlled the town. Robles was convinced to take the job by the local townspeople. The local saloon keeper (Whitney) doesn't care if Robles was the sheriff as long as he was on his payroll.

Katy played Mara Fay in *Dragoon Wells Massacre* 1957, directed by Harold D. Schuster. The movie starred Barry Sullivan, Dennis O'Keefe, Mona Freeman, Sebastian Cabot, and Jack Elam. Captain Matt Riordan (Dennis O'Keefe) was the sole survivor of an Apache attack. A local trader found him. Soon after they were joined by Marshall transporting a wagon load of criminals to court for trial. Later a stagecoach carrying three entertainers joined the strange group. They banded together to get across the desert safely.

Delmer Davis directed her in *The Badlands* in 1958. A western caper film, two ex-inmates discharge their prison sentence and arrived in the town of Prescott. The movie starred Alan Ladd, Ernest Borgnine, Claire Kelly, Kent Smith, and Nehemiah Piersoff. Katy's character was named Anita. She married her co-star Ernest Borgnine on December 31, 1959. Their relationship was very stormy and the couple separated in 1961 amid rumors of spousal abuse and divorced in 1963.

In 1961, she appeared in *One Eyed Jacks,* starring and directed by Marlon Brando. The movie also starred Karl Malden, Ben Johnson, Slim Pickens, Elisha Cook Jr., and Pina Pellicer. Brando, the Kid, and Malden, Dad Longworth, are bandits surrounded by the Juarlies, Dad took the only horse with the promise to get fresh horses and return for Brando. He lied and left the Kid to be caught. After serving five years in prison, Brando

AWARD-WINNING AUTHOR OF *TIN HOLLOW*

# J.B. HOGAN

AVAILABLE IN HARDCOVER, PAPERBACK, AND EBOOK WHEREVER BOOKS ARE SOLD

# MEXICAN SKIES

WWW.THEJBHOGAN.COM

discharged and searched for Dad to kill him for leaving him behind. Katy played Maria Longworth, Dad's wife.

George Sherman directed *Smoky* in 1966. The film starred Fess Parker, Diana Hyland, Hoyt Axton, and Katy as Maria. In the film Parker chased a wild horse named Smoky, he eventually caught and broke the animal. After he went away, the animal is passed around to various owners. When he returned, he discovered the horse pulling a wagon, bought him from the owner and returned him to the wild.

*Stay Away Joe,* released in 1968, is a western comedy directed by Peter Tewksbury. Elvis Presley stared as Native American rodeo rider Joe Lightcloud and Katy played his mother, Annie. The movie also starred Burgess Meredith, Joan Blondell, and L. Q. Jones. Katy broke her foot prior to filming the movie and removed the cast before the break healed, which explained her limp during the movie.

In 1973, she appeared in the film *Pat Garrett and Billy the Kid,* directed by Sam Peckinpah. The film starred Kris Kristofferson, James Coburn, Bob Dylan, and Emilio Fernandez. A long list of character actors appeared in the film, among them, Richard Jaeckel, Chill Wills, Barry Sullivan, Jason Robards, Jack Elam, Slim Pickens, Gene Evans, Paul Fix, Dub Taylor, and R. G. Armstrong. The film chronicles Director Peckinpah's version of the relationship between Pat Garrett (Coburn) and Billy the Kid (Kristofferson). Slim Pickens played Sheriff Colin Baker and Katy played his wife billed as Mrs. Baker. Baker was mortally wounded during a shootout with members of Billy's gang. His wife stayed with him and comforted him as he died. Katy had previously worked with Sam Peckinpah on an episode of *The Rifleman.*

Her final western film was *The High-Lo Country* in 1998. The film starred Billy Crudup, Woody Harrelson, James Gammon, Sam Elliott, Patricia Arquette, and Penelope Cruz. A post World War Two tale about the rivalry between two ranches, Corporate rancher Jim Ed Love and three men, Crudup, Harrelson, and Gammon who employed old school ranching techniques. Katy had a small role as Meesa the witch.

Katy also appeared in several TV shows, during her time in Hollywood. She appeared in the Boardinghouse episode of *The Rifleman* in 1959 with Chuck Connors and Johnny Crawford. In 1960 she appeared with Brian Keith in "Ghost of a Chance," an episode of *The Westerner,* produced and directed by Sam Peckinpah. In 1962 she appeared in the episode "La Tulas" on *Death Valley Days.* She appeared in an episode of *The Virginian* in 1970 titled "The Best Man." Her final appearance on a TV western was in 1972 on *Alias Smith and Jones,* "The McCreede Feud."

In a television interview, Katy stated she met Ernest Borgnine in a restaurant in Mexico when he was in the country filming Vera Cruz in 1954 with Gary Cooper and Burt Lancaster, they married soon after they co-starred in *The Badlands.* She won three Silver Ariel Awards, the Mexican version of the Academy Award for best supporting actress. In 1954 for *El Bruto,* 1974 for *Fe Esperanza y Caridad,* and 1999 for *El Evangelio de cas Maravilles.* Katy was awarded a Golden Boot award in 1992 for her work in western cinema, and a special Golden Ariel in 1997 for Lifetime achievement in film. Her life had several low points. In 1968, Katy attempted to commit suicide, leaving a note behind that said she was too lonely to live. When she recuperated, she left Hollywood and moved back to Mexico. After the death of her son Victor Hugo in 1981, she withdrew from the motion picture community for several years. She died on July 5th, 2002 in Cuernavaca, Morelos, Mexico.

*—Terry Alexander is a western, science fiction and horror writer with many publishing credits to his name. He and his wife, Phyllis, live on a small farm near Porum, Oklahoma.*

# out of the
# CHUTE

**Dennis Doty**

*saddlebag dispatches managing editor*

I got my first cowboy hat when I was five years old. It was a Christmas present. I don't remember who it was from, but most likely it was my paternal grandparents. Grandpa was an old-time cowboy from southeastern New Mexico who had worked on most of the big spreads from the Jingle Bob in his hometown of Roswell all the way up to the Breughmann Brothers' spread outside of Laramie, Wyoming.

It was the typical kid's toy cowboy hat of red felt with wide white laces around the flat brim, but I was proud of that hat. To me, it was never just a prop for playing Cowboys and Indians, although it certainly was used for that. Its real meaning was that I was on the path to being a real life cowboy. I knew all about cowboys. They were tough men who were soft spoken because they didn't have to prove themselves. They had the confidence that comes from knowing that they could get the job done. They treated women, even fancy women, with respect. They didn't take any guff from anyone, always told the truth, and they loved this country with all of their hearts. Oh, and they never cried.

All of my heroes were cowboys. The men I admired and looked up to were men like my Grandpa, John Wayne, Tom Mix, and Roy Rogers. I wanted to be just like them.

It's been over fifty-five years since I got that hat for Christmas, but I still wear one and have for most of those years. There were some years when it wasn't possible. A good hat is expensive and I couldn't always afford one when the old one wore out. Sometimes I had to make do with one made of straw. Sometimes none at all. For ten years, I served in the armed forces and the Marine Corps has its own ideas about proper headgear. I wore the prescribed uniform and was proud of it, but when off duty or off base, I would revert to my personal uniform of jeans, boots, western styled shirt, and cowboy hat. By the time I got out of the military, I wouldn't dream of going outdoors without a hat, and most of the time it was western styled. The hats had become more than a head covering. They were an emblem of a philosophy and lifestyle that I am still proud to embrace.

By then I had two years under my belt on the Southwest rodeo circuit where I learned dozens of increasingly creative and highly entertaining ways to get off of a bucking horse. I also learned that cowboys, even when competing with each other, were always willing to help one another. We talked freely about rodeo stock and how they bucked, which way they were likely to turn out of the chute, how high they would kick. Did this horse sunfish? Did he try to pull extra rein? Was that bull a maneater or was he likely to leave you alone once he got you off? I never once straddled a bucking chute when one or more of my competitors weren't there helping me set my rigging or pull my bull rope tight for me and offering their advice, and I did the same for them.

I've learned that there is a price to pay for this emblem of my lifestyle. I've been called a hick and a hayseed, but you'd better smile when you say it, and those that didn't learned not to say it again. I've learned that

many folks assume that it means I'm uneducated or even unintelligent. I've learned that there's a stigma in the workplace where my hat is frowned upon or even considered unacceptable.

This hat that I wear means that you won't hear me complain about my aches and pains, or my thin wallet, or the lack of groceries in the pantry. It means that I will always give you an honest day's work for a day's pay. It means that when you ask me a question, you're going to get an honest answer. You may not like what you hear, but you can take it to the bank. It means that you will usually find me in church on Sunday morning.

But this hat doesn't always just ride on my head.

> ALL OF MY **HEROES** WERE **COWBOYS**. THE MEN I ADMIRED AND LOOKED UP TO WERE **MEN LIKE MY GRANDPA, JOHN WAYNE, TOM MIX,** AND **ROY ROGERS. I WANTED TO BE JUST LIKE THEM.**

You'll see it tipped forward or doffed completely as I hold a door for a lady. You'll find it over my heart when a funeral procession passes by until the last car has passed. You'll find it there when Old Glory passes or when I hear the Star Spangled Banner. You may find it in my hands but never on my head during a funeral or when I'm praying. You can find it on the seat beside me when I sit up to the table in a restaurant and you'll find it absent when I'm in the house, because this hat knows what respect means.

Over the years, this hat has kept the rain, the sleet and the snow from running down the back of my shirt collar. It keeps the rain and sun out of my eyes. It has provided shade for innumerable naps. It has been a basket for carrying anything from eggs to small animals. Its been knocked off in fights and ground into the dirt of numerous arenas, but I always pick it up and put it back on.

This hat signifies my life-long love of animals, especially dogs and horses. It is symbolic of my understanding that nature, as brutal as it can be at times, is a gift from God. It means that I understand that man never has nor ever will build a cathedral anywhere near as magnificent as the Tetons, and

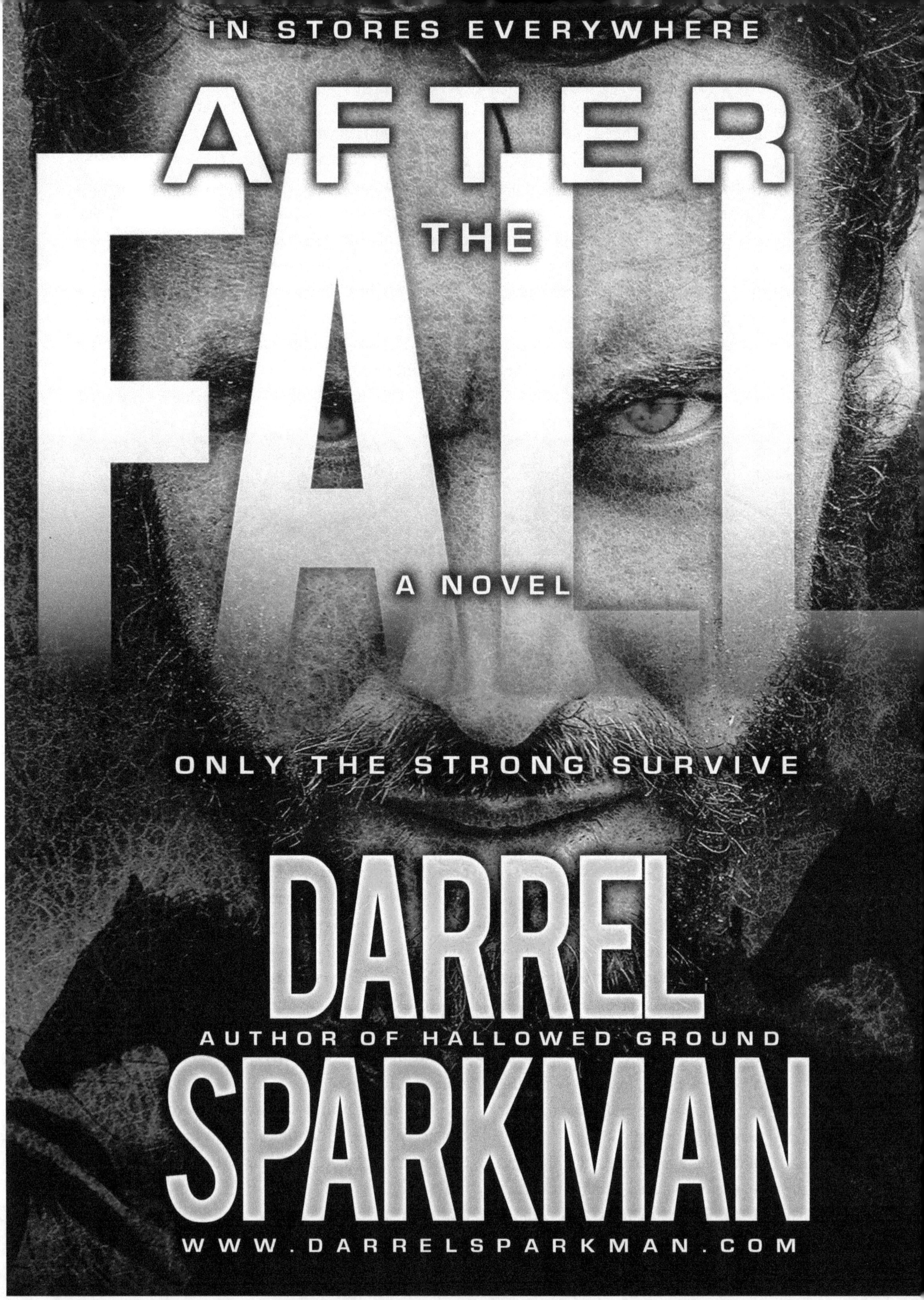

IN STORES EVERYWHERE
AFTER
THE
FALL
A NOVEL
ONLY THE STRONG SURVIVE
DARREL
AUTHOR OF HALLOWED GROUND
SPARKMAN
WWW.DARRELSPARKMAN.COM

I bow my head in reverence when I see what God hath wrought.

Over the years I have learned, to no great surprise, that the cowboy lifestyle which I have tried to live, and which this hat is a symbol of, is extremely inclusive. Almost everyone knows of the Mexican *vaqueros* who were so much a part of our heritage in places like Texas and California. For those of you who don't, they are especially known for their rope work. The *vaqueros* didn't use the twisted rope common on this side of the border which is usually thirty or forty feet long. *Vaqueros* used a *riata*, a braided leather lasso often sixty to eighty feet in length, which required a great deal more skill both in roping a steer and controlling them after the catch. They could rope a steer from fifty feet away and then throw him to the ground with a flick of their wrist. They were real artists.

Many people, nowadays, know that Australia, Brazil, and many other countries produce some of the finest cowboys and rodeo riders on the planet. Fewer know that the old cattle trails were often blazed by black cowboys, men like Bill Pickett who invented bulldogging or Bass Reeves who served as a highly respected Deputy U.S. Marshall under Judge Isaac Parker, policing the Indian Territory from Ft. Smith, Arkansas. Jesse Chisholm, who opened the Chisholm Trail was a mixed blood Cherokee. These men, like all cowboys, were judged not by the color of their skin, but by their honesty and the jobs they did. This is what being a cowboy means.

In the course of the last fifty years, I've learned that one of the things I knew about cowboys as a child was wrong. Cowboys do cry. We cry when death claims a friend. We cry when we find an injured animal. We cry when our troops march by or we see Old Glory wave. We cry when we hear Taps played so mournfully on a trumpet. We even cry when we're forced to watch a chick-flick like *Love Story* or *Titanic.*

I've owned dozens of cowboy hats over the years. I've had white ones, black ones, brown ones. I've had them made from felt, straw, beaver, and even buffalo hair. But no matter what shape, style, or color my hat may be, it will always mean that I am a cowboy and all that it stands for.

Until Next Time,
Dennis W. Doty
*Managing Editor*

# BEST OF THE WEST

**Rod Miller**

*western columnist*

"Westerns" means many things—novels, short stories, poems, TV shows. But, to most, the word conjures up images of cowboys dashing across the silver screen, guns a-blazing in pursuit of the bad guys. It calls to mind panoramic scenery, blue skies framing harsh but beautiful landscapes, like director John Ford's iconic Monument Valley. It's a forum for strong, sometimes sassy, but ultimately submissive women who support their men without question. It means heroes demonstrating undaunted courage, banding together to defeat anti-heroes in violent scenes that result in happy endings.

That basic formula describes countless Western movies that once dominated the big screen and, to a lesser extent, continue to this day. Discussions and debates about which films represent the best of the genre are ubiquitous wherever and whenever fans of the Old West congregate. Every fan has a list of favorites and an accompanying list of reasons why.

For me, no list of the best Western movies would be complete without a film that, against all odds, defies every expectation, every formula, every cliché for a successful Western.

*High Noon*, to my mind, owns a place among the Best of the West.

By 1952, the year *High Noon* was released, most movies were shot in rich color. Not so *High Noon*. Not only is it in black and white, the shades of gray are faded and washed out, with bleached skies and dull shadows. Rather than panoramic landscapes, virtually all the movie takes place on the streets and in the buildings of a small town. The nearest we get to

KELLY AND COOPER IN DEFINING ROLES

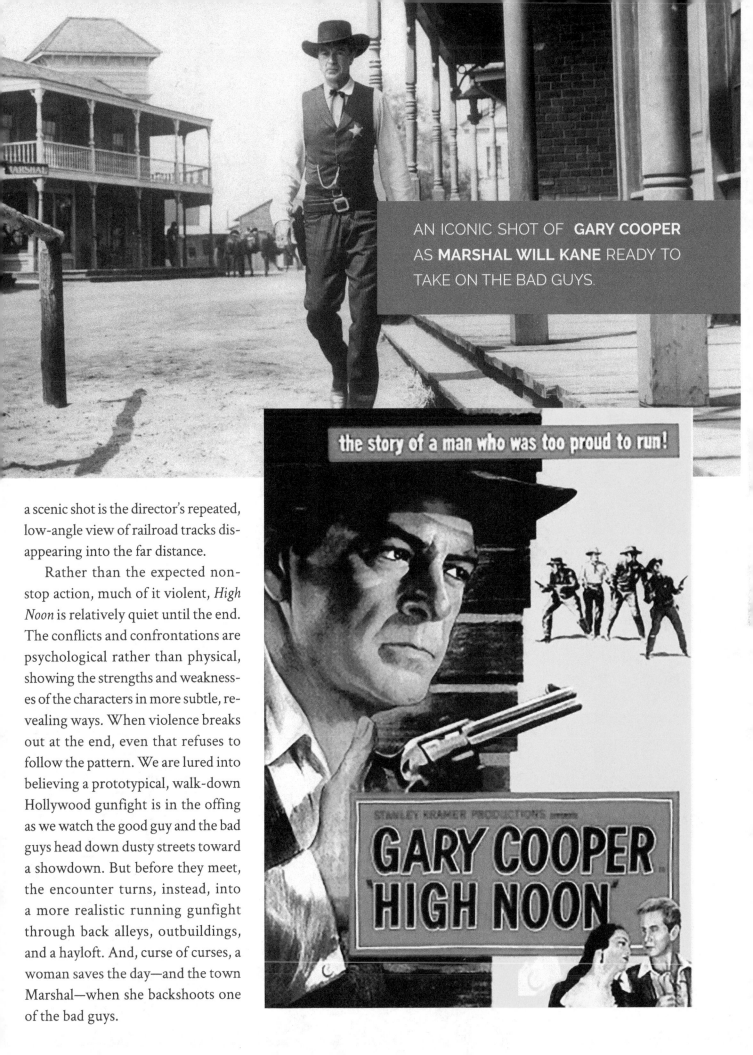

the story of a man who was too proud to run!

STANLEY KRAMER PRODUCTIONS presents

GARY COOPER
HIGH NOON

a scenic shot is the director's repeated, low-angle view of railroad tracks disappearing into the far distance.

Rather than the expected nonstop action, much of it violent, *High Noon* is relatively quiet until the end. The conflicts and confrontations are psychological rather than physical, showing the strengths and weaknesses of the characters in more subtle, revealing ways. When violence breaks out at the end, even that refuses to follow the pattern. We are lured into believing a prototypical, walk-down Hollywood gunfight is in the offing as we watch the good guy and the bad guys head down dusty streets toward a showdown. But before they meet, the encounter turns, instead, into a more realistic running gunfight through back alleys, outbuildings, and a hayloft. And, curse of curses, a woman saves the day—and the town Marshal—when she backshoots one of the bad guys.

OVER **HIGH NOON**'S HOUR-AND-A-HALF RUNNING TIME, WE SEE **COOPER—AS MARSHAL WILL KANE**—START OUT FRESHLY **WASHED AND LAUNDERED** FOR HIS WEDDING TO AMY FOWLER, PLAYED BY GRACE KELLY, **BECOME BATTERED, BLOODY, DIRTY, AND DISHEVELED**. THE PAIN OF A REAL-LIFE BLEEDING ULCER IS EVIDENT ON HIS FACE AS HIS PLEAS FOR HELP IN FACING DOWN THE BAD MEN ARE TURNED DOWN BY ONE AND ALL.

After the climactic battle, the citizens gather in the street to congratulate the victorious lawman. But, rather than the expected, "Aw shucks, 'tweren't nothin', jist doin m' job" conclusion, the Marshal contemptuously tosses his badge into the dirt, climbs onto a buckboard and turns his back on the town and drives away.

While it is a recognized classic among American movies, preserved by the Library of Congress initial entries of significant films in the National Film Registry, not everyone likes *High Noon.* Ever since it was made, the movie has endured repeated attacks for a variety of political, moral, and artistic reasons—particularly from other makers of Westerns. All that is well chronicled so we won't bother with it here.

Plenty of people, however, liked *High Noon.* It was nominated for no less than seven Academy Awards, including Best Picture, and won Oscars for Best Actor, Best Score, Best Song, and Best Editing. The Golden Globe Awards also recognized it with several trophies.

The Best Actor Oscar went to an aging Gary Cooper, who played Will Kane, the beleaguered town Marshal. *High Noon* featured a young Grace Kelly and helped launch her career. Long-time movie villain Lee Van Cleef got his start in the movie, in which he speaks not a word. And work in the movie furthered the careers of several other actors.

*High Noon* was also unusual in that the story unfolds in real time, as we are reminded by the repeated inclusion of clocks in its scenes; clocks that become more prominent as they tick away toward the climactic noon hour. Over the hour-and-a-half, we see Cooper—as Marshal Will Kane—start out freshly washed and laundered for his wedding to Amy Fowler, played by Grace Kelly, become battered, bloody, dirty, and disheveled. The pain of a real-life bleeding ulcer is evident on his face as his pleas for help in facing down the bad men are turned down by one and all.

*High Noon*, without doubt, departs from every expectation for a Western. And that is what makes it the Best of the West.

—*Four-time Spur Award-winning author Rod Miller writes fiction, poetry, and history of the American West and sometimes watches a movie.*

**GARY COOPER** AS **WILL KANE**

**GRACE KELLY** AS **AMY FOWLER**